I0554188

Blood Star

A Space Vampire Novel

Rob Preece

BooksForABuck.com
2017

Chapter One

"Kari. There's something strange outside. You and your sister better to get to safety." Bert Harding's voice in my radio-implant was low, but insistent.

'Outside' meant the near-vacuum of Mjolnir, the small moon where our lab was hidden. Nobody was likely to randomly wander anywhere within a hundred kilometers. Of course, it was completely possible that Harding was pulling a gag.

"Yeah, sure, Mr. Harding," I sent back. Harding was big on having me and my sister run around doing his work for him. I suspected this was just another example.

I'd slaved the lab's proximity warning systems to my implant months earlier so I double-checked to see what Harding was reading. Sure enough, no alarms registered. Harding was a bit of a creep, always staring at me and my sister, so I figured he was probably getting his jollies watching us wiggle into one of our hiding places. Plus, he enjoyed pulling his weight by ordering us around. Still, Harding was in charge of security. If I didn't do what he said, my whole family could get kicked out of the lab. Sure, the lab was a dump. Both the people who worked there and the equipment that kept us alive were rejects nobody else wanted. Which meant, dump or not, we didn't have anyplace else to go.

Maybe Harding had seen something the outside triggers hadn't picked up. The sensors were as trashed as everything else in the lab. Or maybe he'd just got drugged out eating too much of the hasro our lab made. Either way, until I found a way to get off of the lab and on my own, I had to follow orders.

I headed for the hideout I'd discovered inside the oxygen recirculation system. As I ran, I scared up my sister Shena on the phone.

"Harding is weird," she said when I'd relayed the message. "I don't like the way he stares at me."

"He probably just thinks you're a spy."

She giggled. "Like anyone would spy on us."

She had a point. Our lab had to be the least important, least watchable and most boring place in the universe. Still, the Security Corporation didn't like the competition, even from a cut-rate lab like ours. So our boss, Captain Russart, did what he could to keep us low profile and safe.

A minute after I'd burrowed into the soft matting of the scrubbers, my sister piled on top of me. She was eleven and I was fifteen. That, plus the low grav on Mjolnir, meant so she couldn't hurt me no matter how hard she tried but that didn't stop her from trying to knock my wind out. Shena always did her best to be annoying.

"Kari, how come Russart hired Harding anyway?" she whispered. "You did a better job than he ever could."

"Yeah, like anyone will trust a kid with anything important."

"No kidding," Shena said. "It's ridiculous that—"

"Kari." My mother's voice sounded hoarse over the phone. "There's something wrong."

I re-checked with the alarm system artificial intelligence but it showed all systems okay.

"It's probably another of Harding's drills." I'd hate to say that my mother was paranoid, but it seemed I split my life between my father's Kung Fu lessons and my mother's detailed escape plans.

"What drill? There's no notice..." A loud series of coughs cut off whatever she'd intended to say.

"Mother? Are you okay?" We'd been isolated long enough that there was no disease on our lab... so why the coughing?

"Take..." hacking, like she was heaving out the inside of her lungs, "...take care of Shena. You're the strong one."

I hated being the strong one.

Although the atmosphere scrubbing system where we were hiding was pretty dark, I could make out my sister's face. She looked like she was about to be sick. Not a good idea.

Over my radio-implant, I heard more coughing. Then, from my dad, the single word "gas."

Russart took way too many shortcuts, pushing to make quota regardless of safety. Over the three years my parents had worked there, I'd lost count of the times the lab had sprung leaks. We all

4

wore skinsuits all the time, of course. But Russart never bothered supplying gas masks.

I blinked my heads-up alive again, just in case, although surely a spill would have triggered an alarm.

Everything still glowed green. According to the lab's A.I. there wasn't a thing wrong in the universe. Everybody was healthy and all of the equipment was fine.

Except now I heard more coughing. It wasn't just our parents. It seemed to be everyone.

I sat up so quickly I almost got dizzy. Harding had been right and this wasn't a drill.

"I'm scared," Shena allowed.

I'm sure my mother would have told me to comfort her. That wasn't happening. "Yeah," I said. "Me too."

As I watched, one of the green bars twisted red. External failure? Sure the lab could rupture. But that didn't match the coughing or Harding knowing in advance.

"Stay here," I signed rather than spoke. "Keep radio silence and don't make a sound."

If it weren't for the coughing, I would have bet the lab's ancient A.I. was giving us another false alarm. Everything in Captain Russart's rundown lab, definitely including the A.I., had been rejected by somebody else, tossed out to make way for modern equipment, abandoned when the platform's population shrank or emigrated, or been sold at a discount as sub-standard. In a real lab, nobody would have been needed to monitor the systems. Here, though, we had some sort of incident just about every day. In the previous week alone we'd had three filtration malfunctions, which was how I'd found my hiding place in the graphene CO_2 scrubber. We'd also had a major rupture of the lab's exterior skin, venting oxygen to the vacuum outside the station itself, and there was a continual trickle of drug contamination, often leading to temporary poisonings, as just one result of getting by with inadequate manufacturing equipment.

No wonder I wanted out. Not to mention I was tired of working my rear end off for nothing because Russart considered I was just a sort of attachment to my parents… whom he underpaid anyway.

Substandard hardware or not, repair-bots were cheap and Russart hadn't scrimped on them. No matter what disaster hit the lab, the A.I. should have bots in place within seconds, sealing any breaches, cleaning up contamination. No way should an external breach go code-red.

"Stay here," I signed again.

It took less than twenty seconds for me to remove the cover from the air recirculation system, slip out, and re-latch it.

During that time, though, the sounds of coughing faded. That had to be good news, right?

I re-checked my display, hoping to see the indicators flickering back to green.

The reds, and there were more of them now, were slowly flashing out but I didn't get any comfort from that. They weren't going back to amber or green. They were going black. Which meant system shut-down.

Then the rest of them went black at once—at the same time as an annoying buzz filled the lab.

I recognized the high-pitched zing—slow, slow, quick-quick. Everyone knew this alarm. Everyone dreaded it. We were venting atmosphere to space and someone, or something, was coming in.

I almost called Harding but he could hear the alarm as well as I could and radio silence might be important. For sure he had to have his hands full.

I sucked in as much oxygen as I could before it was gone. I didn't have much hope of doing anything useful if the lab's repair-bots couldn't handle the breach, but I made my way to the central console anyway.

The lab's lights went out before I'd taken ten steps, replaced by the underpowered emergency system—I remembered my mother complaining about Russart diverting emergency power to help churn out more Hasro but hadn't really thought about the consequences. Of course, nobody expects multiple catastrophic system failure.

Although the emergency system lighting was dim, it shed enough photons for me to make my way across the floor.

I stumbled over something as I reached the console but I ignored whatever it was and slapped the override buttons to rev up atmosphere generation, flush toxins and reboot the artificial intelligence.

Only when I'd taken care of basic emergency procedure did I look around.

I'd missed my adult eye implants when I hit twelve—I was small for my size and my parents were saving money. Which meant I couldn't see much into the infrared spectrum. So it seemed strange that I could see anything at all when the emergency lighting went black.

Being able to see in near-pitch darkness wasn't what I wanted right then. Because what I saw in the putrid glow put out by the emergency systems was too horrid.

Bodies lay strewn around the lab floor. The thing I'd stumbled over on my way to the control board turned out to be my mother... or rather her body. She lay in a pool of blood.

Seeing that black blood made me dizzy so tried not to think and just let my training do its job. I reached for her throat, desperately feeling for a pulse.

Nothing.

Can't be, I promised myself. I wiggled my fingers. It was getting cold in the dark lab. Maybe I'd missed her artery. Maybe I needed to try harder. Maybe…

"Come on." My voice sounded squeaky and weak in the thinning atmosphere. "You've got to be all right."

She wasn't all right though, and she didn't reply.

This was more important than any security risk. I broke radio silence to emergency-link from my implant to hers, signaling it to take her into life-preservation mode, shutting down unnecessary systems and pumping what blood she had to the brain.

Mom's implant signal was weak. All I could get from it was that she'd suffered multiple simultaneous organ failure. But it did confirm it was activating emergency mode.

A part of me wanted to stay by her side, howl at Thor overhead, rage against an unfair universe. But both my parents had raised me to respond to crisis through action.

She must have known she was dying when she'd told me to take care of Shena. Instead of following her last wishes, I'd abandoned my sister.

Turned out, all those drills she'd taken us through hadn't been so silly after all. They were finally going to come in handy… if I hadn't already ruined everything.

I'll take care of Shena, I mentally promised the corpse that had been my mother. *You've got my word.*

I'd already broken radio silence once, so I figured it couldn't hurt to do it again. My sister had a bad habit of following me around and I definitely didn't want her to see this. "Stay quiet and stay hidden," I radioed to Shena. "I'm coming back as soon as I can." At least the atmosphere scrubbing plant was probably the safest place in the lab for her to wait.

Then I switched off my radio implant.

"Okay." The sound of my own voice startled me and only partly because of the squeaky sound. "Think, don't just react."

I needed to get back to Shena, but first, I needed to get my mother to cryo. If I could get her frozen in time, the hospital on Gardenia should be able to revive her. We'd be in debt for the rest of our lives from what they'd charge us, but at least she'd be alive.

I ignored the dizzy feeling I got when I stood, figuring I could deal with my shock later. My mother was bigger than me but Mjolnir didn't have much gravity so when I grabbed her under her armpits and dragged her toward the emergency cryo system, her body came along. I'd just made it to the hatch when my heads-up went into display mode without authorization.

Multiple organ failure.

It took me a long second to realize what I was seeing. This wasn't my mother's failure report—it was mine.

I tried to turn around but my legs had stopped listening and I pitched forward into the cryo.

The last thing I saw, as my consciousness faded, was the black uniform of the Security Corporation.

Security was never good news, especially for a lab that violated station rules. Still, any help was better than dying there. I needed to tell them about my mother. They would surely shut down the lab so I needed to let them know where Shena was hiding. I needed…

Then I didn't think any more.

****

8

"Well, will you look at this?"

Normally when someone talks, I open my eyes and pretend to pay attention. My father used to slap me in the head when I didn't show him what he called "respect," and what I called, but only in my own mind, "slavish devotion."

I didn't recognize this voice, which was odd considering only twelve people lived at the lab and I knew all of them. Still, something in the male speaker's tone warned me to stay calm and listen.

"Lab results finally in?" The second voice was female but it sounded just as indifferent.

"Could have saved us a lot of work if we'd gotten them earlier."

"You mean she's—"

"No, she's not dead. Yet. Might as well be, though. She got a good dose of the gas. I guess she's at that, well, uncomfortable age."

"You mean... oh, no." For the first time I thought I heard compassion in the woman's voice. "She looks so young. She doesn't even have her adult implants."

"I'm sure that's why they brought her in. Fooled them too but it turns out she's a teen."

A long pause. I came up empty when I tried to call the heads-up from my implants, so I used a meditation I'd learned during kung-fu practice to steady my pulse and keep my breathing slow and even.

"At least she hasn't wakened," the female said. "I don't know if I could terminate a kid once I'd talked with her."

Terminated? I didn't like that word, especially in connection with me.

"She's not a kid anymore."

"Still looks like one. You know, I just don't—"

"Don't even think that way or you'll be as dead as she is. Besides, *we* don't have to do anything. We'll message Security that we're ready for them to pick up their merchandise. When they get here, I'll let them know the details."

"Oh, that's brilliant. You tell them she's you-know-what before we hand her over and they'll find some reason they can't stop by."

"So we keep that part a secret." The male sounded cheerful. "No reason for us to worry about terminating the little thing. We tell Security when they show up and it's their job—they'll have to handle the dirty work. In the meantime, we can get back to our job healing actual people."

"I guess that should be comforting."

It didn't seem comforting to me.

"I hate those—"

"Don't even say the word. You don't think Security A.I. monitors for key tags? Just let it go."

The voices moved on, but I waited another minute before cautiously opening one eye.

I'd never been in a hospital before, but I'd seen plenty of tri-Ds. The blinking monitors, the ozone stink, and the white sheets weren't exactly the same as those in the tri-ds. For one thing, this wasn't as clean and organized. Still, it didn't take any great genius to realize I'd somehow ended up in a major medical clinic.

When I remembered the last read-out on my pop-up, I realized I shouldn't be too surprised. A hospital was the best chance after multiple organ failure.

Recalling that display made me remember the rest of it—my mother's body lying on the floor, almost but not quite to the cryo, the harsh buzz of the intrusion alarm and ... and my sister hiding in the air filtration system.

For a moment I let myself hope. They'd found me in the cryo near my mother. If they'd brought me, maybe they'd brought her.

But there wasn't much market for full-grown adults and we didn't have much money in our account, not hospital-paying money. Which meant Security probably wouldn't bother bringing mom in, even if it hadn't been too late. I tried to remember where my father had been before Harding had called in his warning and decided he'd been in the Hasro lab. It would take a miracle for either of them to have gotten away.

Thinking about my family messed with my meditation and my heart started pounding uncomfortably.

Once the emergency hit the lab, I'd been responsible for two things. First, my mother had told me to take care of Shena. Second,

I'd needed to get my mother frozen before her death could become permanent. I'd failed at both of them.

A part of me wanted to give up. After all, what could Security do to me that would make matters worse? Then, even though my radio implant was inoperative, I somehow heard the echo of my mother's voice in my head. "You're the strong one."

Yeah, right. I was so strong I didn't know if I could lift the sheet off my hospital bed.

A picture of Shena popped into my head. She'd be hiding and waiting in the atmosphere scrubber, certain I'd return to rescue her. She'd be getting cold but the scrubber would retain enough oxygen to keep her alive for days even if the lab was completely without power. I didn't have time to lie in a hospital bed feeling sorry for myself. Maybe there was nothing I could do for my mother. Maybe my father had gotten caught in the disaster as well. I'd mourn them later. For now, though, I was going to do what I could for my sister.

I looked around, moving just my eyes. A physical call button, glowing bright red, was within easy reach. In a weak moment, I stretched my hand toward it. Remembering those doctors talking about termination made me yank my hand back. Right then, they were calling Security in to deal with me so they wouldn't have to kill me themselves. If they knew I was awake, they'd tell Security to hurry. Or maybe they'd just overcome their scruples. Either way, I was dead.

I ignored the part of me that wanted to give up. I'd promised my mother I'd take care of Shena and I intended to do just that. First, though, I had to get away from the hospital and back to the lab.

From what I'd seen in the vids, the first thing they do in the hospital is slave your implant to their systems. That lets them monitor and regulate your heartbeat, detect any failures, and pump you with whatever drugs their A.I. decides you need. The process also cuts off voluntary muscle control, which means a patient can't just get up and walk away.

Still, my hand had jerked just slightly when I'd seen the call button. And I was pretty sure I'd voluntarily opened my eyes. Could my implants have failed as a result of my cryonic failure rather than from the hospital's hacking?

11

Despite an irrational fear that if I shut my eyes they'd stay shut, I tried a blink.

Success.

Next, I tried moving a finger. That worked too.

I checked everywhere I could without moving my head, then ran my right hand down my body.

I was in the standard jell-bath bed, completely naked beneath the decorative white sheet that provided minimal decency. From what I could tell, I wasn't physically attached to anything.

A lot of the supplies we got at lab came shipped in jell, so I knew to move in it … slowly. Jells are designed to prevent impact damage, so the harder you push, the more firmly they push back.

At the back of my brain, some part of me kept shouting to hurry, to get away from there before Security came. My sense of being lost in the world without my parents added to the panic. But I forced myself to stay calm as I gently eased my way free from the sticky stuff.

People are supposed to get their adult software upgrades for their implants when they turn twelve. Shena would have gotten hers on her birthday, a week away and I would have gone along and gotten mine at the same time, my parents lying about my age. Even the kid version has a lot of features, though. I depended on mine for a heads-up display monitoring my health, tracking the time I spent in the centrifuge to keep my muscles and bones from atrophying, sending videos, talking, watching tri-ds, and just about everything else. Losing it added to the weight of losing everything else.

Losing my implant did have a couple of advantages. First, it meant that the hospital wasn't using it to monitor me and couldn't use it to track me if I got out. Second, if it were working, I'd monitor my condition and, when I did I'd get a visual reminder of finding my mother and then failing to get her to cryo in time.

Thinking of my mother stalled me for a second, and during that moment I gave up a bit of the progress I'd made through the jell. So I forced the memories right back down. My parents had made some bad decisions and had nothing but rotten luck all their lives, but they were my parents and I didn't want to remember them lying on the ground, their lungs and blood coughed out around them. For sure, I didn't want to play back any video of finding them that way.

Getting free seemed to take forever, but finally I stood beside the hospital bed, gently tugging free my right arm—the last part of me embedded in the jell.

The jell gave a hiss when my arm came free.

I was completely naked, so I yanked the decorative sheet off the jell-bed, wrapped it around myself, and took a big step toward the EXIT sign.

That's when a thought hit me. Clearly the doctors had been horrified by whatever had happened to me. Maybe I had some contagious disease that might infect the entire station. Maybe alien babies had embedded themselves in my stomach and would burrow their way out through my guts and skin when they became viable. At any rate, I needed to know why my implant had told me my body had gone through major organ failure and figure out whether I was going to go out and kill everyone.

With my implant off-line, I couldn't read the memory stick at the foot of the jell-bed but I grabbed it anyway. When I got my systems working again, I'd scan it and figure out what had the doctors so bent. I just had to hope I wouldn't kill everyone in Gardenia before I had that chance.

Only when I had the memory stick firmly in hand did I head for the exit.

Chapter Two

People said that our lab stank.

It hadn't seemed that bad to me: maybe because I was used to it or maybe because my implant had been programmed to set the odors of sweating humans, recycled air, and failing electronics as normal. There was no mistaking the miasma of whatever pit I'd fallen into in the misnamed Gardenia, though. This was truly rank.

I hadn't been into Gardenia, the only real town on the mini-moon Mjolnir, for nearly a year. Back then, we hadn't stayed in the nicer areas, but at least it had been clean.

I choked down a sob when I remembered my family had planned to come to Gardenia in just a few days for my sister's and my adult implant upgrades. Mom had talked about a 'real' vacation together although I had no idea how we would afford it. Instead of a family vacation in a mid-priced hotel, I huddled alone, behind a slag pile with severe halitosis, and wondered where to go next.

The name Gardenia was supposed to evoke the idea of a beautiful garden. The reality: not so much. Like the entire mined-out moon on which it sat, Gardenia had already been a pit when my family had arrived on Mjolnir orbit more than a decade earlier. From the looks of the slum outside the hospital, things had gotten worse. Lots worse.

The planetoid wasn't completely devoid of beauty. Overhead, Thor, the gas giant Mjolnir orbited, gleamed red and purple—an impressive vision even through the scratched and battered diamond dome that kept Gardenia's fouled atmosphere from drifting off into space.

Light from Asgard, the distant sun, provided a gentle and constant glow as it refracted off millions of orbital solar collectors that theoretically grabbed every erg of power that reached them in the ever-more difficult task of suppling visiting ships and keeping the platform alive one more day.

Many of the structures inside the dome had been constructed with stark lines and sharp angles that would have been impossible except in microgravity. Some even retained artistic embellishments going back to the days when Gardenia was rich, the center of trade for a dozen star systems, and a growing hub.

Although spots of beauty remained, they didn't even come close to hiding the ugly. The orbital power arrays covered the heavens, but half those systems were out of phase or had been damaged by collisions or solar storms. From what my parents told me, Security refused to let anyone replace the defective ones without paying a fine many times higher than the launch cost. Instead of being a gleaming vision of light, Gardenia sat in perpetual dusk, its temperatures hovering at a miserable chill just above the freezing point of water... or blood.

While Gardenia was faded, it remained an active refining site and the road where I huddled served as a route for minerals destined for the refineries. Without my implant working, I used the rumble of ore transports to judge the passage of time.

The dust those transports raised hung in the air, then slowly dispersed, with Brownian motion spreading the filth throughout the city, creating layer after layer of grime everywhere I could see.

From time to time as I peeked from my hiding place behind what had been the doorway to an abandoned shop, I caught sight of other humans—mostly peering out of windows or half-closed doors. Like the structures and the trash, the people too seemed covered by layers of slowly falling dust.

At first, I thought those searching eyes might be looking for me. The hospital might have put out some notice of an escaped patient, especially if I had some weird contagious disease that implants couldn't cope with. But people looking for escaped, dangerous prisoners should have expressions on their faces—whether hopeful of reward, fearful of contagion or *something*. These people were just staring. As my panic subsided, I realized most of them didn't know what they were looking for—and wouldn't recognize it if self-adhered to their hands. All had the glazed look of the Hasro addict. Hasro, the drug we'd manufactured at the lab, was the crutch of choice for everyone living in a depressing or hopeless situation. The drug enhanced sensitivity to the implant, letting the user taste wonderful cuisine when eating the gruel their constructors extruded, see fairy castles instead of slums built out of refinery slag, and experience magnificent passion when viewing a cheap tri-D. That last, at least, was what my friend Jack, with the experience of his seventeen years, had told me. My parents had just told me to stay away from both Hasro and the cheap tri-Ds, although we'd had enough lab accidents and spills to give everyone more than a taste of the drug's effects. When I asked them why they spent their lives working in an unlicensed Hasro plant if the drug was too dangerous for me to use, they'd explained that people were going to use it and they were undermining Security's Hasro prices, making them like Robin Hood. I hadn't been convinced. I suspected they'd taken the only jobs they could find. It wasn't as if Mjolnir system offered a lot of choices.

As I shivered under the hospital sheet I'd wrapped around my scrawny body, I wondered if the people wandering around with blank looks saw beautiful skyscapes rather than grime and filth. I also wondered how they saw me. Was I a fairy princess? Or maybe a monster?

With only the sheet wrapped around my body, I'd stand out if I left my hiding spot. But I couldn't stay so close to the hospital. Sooner or later, Security would come looking.

What I needed was an ally, someone who knew her way around Gardenia. Someone who had access to medical facilities so I could re-install my implants, maybe even figure out a way to get the adult upgrade. And most of all, I had to find someone who could help me get back to the lab to dig out Shena before it was too late. But who could I trust? Who would want to help an escapee from the hospital, especially one the cops were hunting?

I waited until I saw a kid, maybe a year or so older than my own fifteen, skulk out of one of the structures carrying what looked like a couple of meal-sticks.

He was skinny, with ribs sticking out under a thin gray shirt. His dark hair flopped forward mostly covering eyes that darted everywhere, as if he expected someone to grab him. Despite his dark hair, his skin was pale—Gardenia's dome and the solar collectors kept out most radiation. From the grease-caked dirt on his knees and backside, I figured he didn't have a regular place to wash or sleep.

Approaching him could be the last mistake I ever made.

I took another look at his food-sticks. My stomach growled.

"You gonna share that," I whispered as I slunk behind him. "Or do I have to report you for thieving?"

He jumped like I'd hit him with a shock-prod. "I didn't do nothing. It's my food."

I'd just been guessing he'd stolen the food. When he lied, I knew I was right.

I grinned at him. "Your food? Oh, yeah. Right. No problem then. Security checks you out, sees that you're just minding your own business with your own property and pats you on the head and sends you on your way. You've got nothing to worry about. Unless you're lying, of course. Then—"

He shook his shaggy head. "Security comes, they'll take you first. You're a girl."

He had a point. Security had to turn a profit like anyone else, and they lowballed their oversight-and-monitoring bids on places like Gardenia precisely because they expected some chances to grab merchandise. From what my parents had told me, a fifteen-year-old girl wasn't worth what a twelve-year-old could bring but she still had some value. Security would catch me and sell me … unless they killed me first.

"Guess we'd both be better off if Security stays far away," I admitted.

"Pretty much always a good idea."

I didn't need my implant to get the flashback of those black uniform trousers I'd seen when I'd fallen into the cryo, my brain managed that all by itself. I'd thought 'Security' then and I still thought so. Which made some sense. Maybe our Hasro lab hadn't been Robin Hood, but security was still the Sheriff of Nottingham. They didn't want anyone else grabbing any of the drug money.

"Need you to scan something for me." I shoved the memory strip I'd pulled off my hospital bed in his direction.

He stared at it like it might jump out of my hand and bite him. "Why don't *you* do it? Trying to infect me with something?"

"I can't scan it myself. My systems got scrambled is all. You can see the strip is from the hospital—they're about curing, not giving you an implant virus."

He gave me a speculative look. A homeless kid would be looking for a way to make some money and he wouldn't have to go to Security to find a market for a teenage girl. If he knew the right people, he could probably trade me for a month's supply of Hasro. Of course, he had to know where … and have a lot of trust. People who would pay for me would take a teenage boy as well. There were plenty of customers for both.

"All right." He held out a dirty hand. "Give me the strip."

I prepared for him to grab me. When that didn't happen, I handed over the plastic data store.

He ran a finger over it, sucking the information into his implant, then rolling back his eyes as he checked it out on his heads-up. "Okay," he said. "Looks like you were hospitalized with a severe … oh, hell."

He dropped his food-sticks and backed away.

"What?"

"Nothing."

I tackled him as he turned to run, falling on top of him. The food he'd stolen rolled away, but food was tough. We could dust it off and eat it later.

I'm a girl and not especially big for my age. The boy had six inches on me and, while he was skinny, he also had *some* muscle. I thought he should fight better, at least give me a challenge.

To make matters worse, my sheet came off in the scramble.

He looked up at me like I was something out of a horror tri-d. "Don't hurt me."

"Tell me what it says."

"It says you're supposed to be terminated."

"Terminated, not enslaved?"

The doctors had said something like that but hearing it from the kid made it official. Security hadn't killed me when they'd raided our lab because they'd thought I was worth something. But they'd been wrong. Why wasn't I worth anything, though? Yeah, I was skinny and looked enough like a kid my parents had saved on getting adult implants, but some gross people paid for that kind of look. I tried to think of any diseases that would cost more to cure than a slave would be worth and came up empty. "Why?" I demanded.

The kid shook his head. "Who'd dare enslave a vampire?"

****

There was no such thing as a real vampire—like in the tri-ds. Even with modern sculpts, people still couldn't turn into bats. As for flying, there was nothing to it. Just about anyone on a low-grav planet or ship could fly... as long as they weren't in a spin-up zone. And nobody was idiot enough to make themselves so light sensitive they'd turn to dust if hit by a few stray UV rays. What there was turned out to be close enough, though. Modern vampires had a disease and needed a steady supply of human blood to keep healthy. According to the kid, I was now one of them. From everything I'd heard, vampires weren't sold as slaves. They were... we were hunted for sport and for the bounty Security put out for us.

For the past couple of years, tri-ds had shown constant variations of brave Security agents battling hordes of blood-sucking vampires. The news was filled with stories of vampire invasion, attacks on humans and especially on medical facilities where blood might be kept and where their potential victims would be unable to fight back, strapped down in jell-beds with their implants slaved to the hospital's A.I. No wonder the doctors had been afraid of me.

In all those tri-ds, both the outright fictional and the supposedly factual, vampires were a mystery—they'd just started appearing out of nowhere. Thanks to the kid's reading of the data stick, though, I had a pretty good idea how they'd got their start. Whatever attack weapons Security used to clean out unauthorized labs had killed the others and caused my condition.

Captain Russart had warned us about Security's latest tool—a custom virus designed specifically to kill adults but not the children—who were then sold into slavery. He'd claimed he'd sprung for the heavy-duty filters and that his new assistant, Bert Harding, was some sort of expert at combatting the virus. I wondered if Security had tracked Harding's purchases, creating the very problem he'd been trying to prevent. At fifteen, I wasn't an adult, but I wasn't a kid either. Apparently Security's attack virus had thought I was somewhere in between 'spare' and 'kill.' According to legend, vampires, as a sort of undead, were supposed to between alive and dead so I guessed it made a sick kind of sense.

"I'm new to this." I stayed on top of the kid and twisted his arm behind his back. "Does the data strip say anything else?"

"Uh, could you get off of me?"

"Oh, that would be smart. I get off and you run away. You want me to let you go, you answer my questions first."

He shook his head. "No way would I run. A vampire could hunt me down and swallow me before I moved two steps. Just like you did a second ago."

I was busy trying not to panic about being a vampire but his saying that word out loud startled me. Still, I wondered if the tri-ds were right, if I'd become faster. Or maybe stronger. I didn't notice any differences but the dirty kid wouldn't know that.

"Answer my questions," I said, "and I'll think about letting you survive."

"Uh, you're naked." He seemed embarrassed by this fact.

He couldn't be half as embarrassed as I was, but that didn't mean I was going to let him get away.

"If I'm a vampire, that means I'm not human. You shouldn't care whether I have clothes on or not. Are you some kind of sicko or something, wanting to mess around with non-humans?"

He looked confused. "Maybe you're not human. But, ah, you're still a girl."

I couldn't argue with that—I was a girl, but I was so skinny I hardly had any figure at all—a combination of the workout routines my father had insisted on and a tiny mother. So, it wasn't as if I came over-endowed with the body parts that guys supposedly found so distracting. Still, it was embarrassing to be naked in front of a boy and humiliating to have him remind me about it.

A part of me wanted to grab the sheet and hide. But this wasn't just about me. I'd promised my mother I'd take care of my sister and that wasn't going to get done if I hid somewhere waiting for Security to hunt me down and execute me.

Right now, I needed to figure out how to stay alive long enough to help Shena. Which meant pretending the whole naked thing wasn't happening.

"What else does the memory stick say?"

It turned out it said a lot. Specifically, the virus had killed my body's ability to create white blood cells, which meant, if I didn't get a regular infusion, I'd catch every disease out there and die. Fortunately, the jell I'd been soaking in had loaded me with antibodies so I was okay for the moment. I wondered, though, how long that would last. Without my implant, I had no way of knowing.

Still, the scientific language on the memory stick comforted me a little. Being a vampire didn't make me a monster the way the tri-ds showed. How was needing a regular fix of fresh blood different from being hooked on Hasro, except Hasro made people happy and white blood cell transfusions only kept people alive?

When the kid had given me everything that sounded useful off the memory stick, I got off of him and grabbed my sheet.

I expected him to run away but instead he gathered up the food-sticks he'd dropped. He broke one in half, and handed the smaller chunk to me. The look he gave me was truly weird. Then again, how was he supposed to look at a vampire?

"What?"

"Can you, maybe, put on the sheet?"

I covered up, but the wrap remained an obvious hospital sheet, which simply screamed that it was out of place here.

"You have anything else I can wear?"

He shook his head. "Do I look like I drag a wardrobe behind me?"

"I'm Kari, by the way."

"Ronin."

"As in some kind of unemployed samurai?" Like most of us, Ronin was a sort of ethnic mix. He might have some Japanese in him, but there was a lot of other stuff, too, giving him both dark hair and pale gray eyes. Under other circumstances, I would have thought he was cute. With my sister's life hanging in the balance and my new status, I wasn't going to waste time thinking about physical looks.

He shrugged. "Apparently my parents were fans of old tri-ds. That a problem for you?"

"No problem, just checking. Anyway, you have a knife?"

He backed off like I'd threatened him.

"Not to slice your arteries with," although I would need to figure out a way to get some blood eventually. Those hospital antibodies wouldn't last forever. "To fix up my sheet."

"Tell me where you want it sliced."

He didn't have a knife but he had a little laser-cutter. On my instructions, he carved out a round head-hole in the center of the sheet.

When I put my newly created poncho on, it felt like a tent. I wasn't sure it was much of an improvement from the standpoint of looking like a hospital sheet, but at least it wouldn't fall off every time I moved.

Ronin sighed when I covered myself up. I wasn't the most beautiful female in the world and my figure hadn't developed much yet—at least I'd hoped there was more development to come back when I imagined living more than another day or two. Still, I'd never thought of myself as scary-ugly before. Then again, I'd never thought of myself as a vampire, either.

"Looks like you're wearing something you stole from a fat lady," he admitted.

That made me feel better ... not. "Yeah?" I said. "Well, I'm not exactly a tailor."

He unfastened his belt and I got a little nervous. What happened to him being afraid of the big mean vampire?

"Hey. What do you think—"

He handed over the belt, then stepped quickly away. "Put this on and tighten it up. Maybe it'll, you know, make it look like you're wearing some sort of toga or something. Still odd considering most everyone wears skintights, but not as noticeable."

"Maybe." I followed his instructions. The thin fabric of the sheet clung to me, which wasn't exactly modest. But he was right—with the belt, the whole thing looked a lot more like a badly designed dress and less like a hospital sheet. That was an improvement.

"Okay," I said. "Thanks for your help and for the food-stick. I'm going to be leaving now."

Again, he surprised me. "Where are you going to go? With no implant, you won't be able to contact anyone, you won't be able to pay for anything, you won't be able to use transportation."

He was right, but that didn't mean I could tell him where I was going. By now, Security would have learned that I'd gotten away. I suspected they'd post a reward. Ronin couldn't collect it himself—Security would snag a cute kid for their own purposes instead of paying him. But Ronin couldn't have survived for long without making contacts who could.

All of which made telling him my plans very dangerous.

"I'm a vampire, remember. You should be thanking your lucky stars I'm letting you walk away. After all, I am hungry." I tried to stick my canines out. "And not just for a food-stick."

He nodded. "You got problems, I got problems. We stick together, maybe we can help each other."

"What sort of problems do you have?" I *really* didn't need anything new to worry about.

He ignored my question. "And the way I see it, you're going to have to deal with the whole blood feeding thing. Right?"

"Why? You offering?"

He took a step backward, shaking his head. "People look at me and they're suspicious. A kid, by himself, is either trouble or he's prey. A pair of teens together, though, could be a young couple on a date. We could be shopping or looking for an apartment. And besides, no offense…"

He trailed off, which meant he knew I'd be offended by whatever came next.

"All right," I said. "I won't bite your head off. What?"

He flinched when I used the word "bite" but he didn't back off and I liked that. "You're a girl. We pull a scam together and people will get looking at you, thinking about whether they could grab you and, you know, sell you or keep you for themselves. While they're doing that, they won't pay no attention to me. Not as much, anyway. If I happen to grab a food-stick, or some other swag, they won't notice."

"Unless they've got their A.I. watching."

"Yeah. Can't get away from that, can we? But where I'm talking about, people don't like A.I.s watching them, know what I mean?"

"You're crazy. Everyone has A.I.s."

He shook his head. "Not the bars where sailors hang out."

He took his laser-cutter and trimmed my sheet so it showed my knees and half my thighs. "They get off their ships flush with cash—the kind they can spend without an I.D. because they want to buy things Security can't officially approve of but doesn't bother preventing either. Hasro and girls and alcohol."

"But—"

"So here's what we'll do. You promise them girly action, make them come out with you to some hidden place where nobody can see. When you've got them distracted, I come up behind and bash them over the head. We split any cash, I get like jewels or whatever, you drink their blood, I pay off what I owe, and we both stay free and alive."

"You'd kill them?"

He giggled. "Gotta kill them, what else? I mean, if you just rob them, they'll run to Security. And Security doesn't like it when freelancers mess with sailors. If Security gets on our trail, then we're the ones dead."

Ronin's plan sounded incredibly dangerous, not to mention stupid. First, everyone knew sailors traveled together, including when they took girls. Second, Security cared more about protecting sailors than they did locals because Gardenia needed shipping more than the shippers needed Gardenia. If the sailors didn't think Security's A.I.s would be watching, they were wrong. And third, it sounded like *I'd* be the one who'd be in trouble if anyone got caught. If nothing else, Security would pull up pictures of me from the dead sailors' implants when it recovered the bodies.

"You can't drink blood from locals," Ronin reminded me. "People would complain. Nobody would notice if a few sailors went missing, though."

Should the idea of killing strangers bother me? I wondered. After all, I was a vampire—I was supposed to be evil and blood-thirsty.

I told myself couldn't kill anyone just to drink his blood. When I got really thirsty, though, I wondered if, maybe, I would change my mind.

Chapter Three

I didn't trust Ronin. Even if I got desperate enough to agree to his plan, which wasn't happening, I couldn't be confident he would come through on his end of the bargain. It was one thing to talk about sneaking up on sailors and bashing them. Actually doing it was something else. And the only thing scarier than Security after me for killing Sailors was Sailors *and* Security coming after me for failing to kill them.

Still, I couldn't get too mad at the kid just for suggesting we roll a few sailors. And forcing him to go away didn't seem wise. For one thing, he had a point about two people working together. For another, as long as I was on his side, he'd have one less reason to sell me to Security.

Still, I wasn't a criminal, which I explained to him.

"Of course you're a criminal." The phony patience in Ronin's voice reminded me of my mother. And right then, I didn't need the reminder. Every minute I spent here doing nothing, Shena was getting hungrier, getting more scared, and getting more likely to do something stupid. Which I'd promised my mother I'd stop her from doing.

"Listen," I said, "I haven't—"

"You just ate half a stolen food-stick, right?"

I looked down and noticed the bar he'd handed me was gone.

"You said it wasn't stolen. And anyway—"

"Like you believed me. Try not to be such a liar. Besides, before you became a vampire, you were working in an unlicensed drug lab, right?"

"Security has no legal right to monopolize Hasro. We help people who need their medicine and otherwise couldn't—"

"Blah blah blah. You're violating Security regulations which means you're a criminal. It doesn't matter that you try to justify it. And one last thing, you're a vampire. Which everyone knows is—"

"But I haven't sucked anyone's blood. I'm a potential vampire, not an actual—"

He shook his head. "Doesn't matter. Still a terminal crime."

"So you're saying that once Security classifies me as criminal, I can do whatever I want? Basic morality doesn't apply to me?"

"They don't just *classify* you as criminal. You *are* a criminal. And they execute vampires on sight."

I didn't owe Security anything. That didn't mean I could justify murdering them, let alone innocent drunk sailors, just to take their money and blood.

"If you meet an innocent sailor," Ronin said, when I'd told him that "let everyone know. Because he'll be the first."

From the tri-ds, I suspected Ronin had a point. But I had a better idea than killing sailors. I had to get back to the lab, find Shena, and protect her. Unless Security was really thorough, there were assets in the lab I could use to help me and Shena get away. I could even give Ronin something to pay off whatever he owed.

"Forget the killing," I said. I need to make sure my sister's okay. Once I do that, I can help you."

"If she was wherever you are, she's dead now. It's only because you're so young that you survived. Uh, sort of."

Yeah, I got that people didn't think vampires were completely alive. I felt alive, though. And I wanted to keep it that way.

"She was hidden in the air filtration system," I said. "I told her to stay put. It's got to be the safest place in the lab. She's probably still hidden."

He shook his head. "A hidden dead sister is no better off than if she'd been found. And another vampire is at least two too many."

"She's younger than me. The gas wouldn't kill her—Security wants to enslave the young ones. Don't you get it? Vampire is a side effect of the poisons. Gotta be."

He nodded slowly. "Yeah, us in-between ages don't have as much value so they wouldn't care about us."

I couldn't argue with that. I didn't know why adults hated teens, but that was the way things worked. And turning us into vampires was only the latest in what they did to us.

"But," he continued, "what if they—"

"Look, I need to know if my sister is alive or dead, captured or free. Like I said, I can't do anything else until I find out. Besides, if the lab is empty, we can loot it."

He sighed. "Tell me where your lab is."

****

"How the heck are we supposed to travel halfway across Mjolnir with Security after us?" Ronin was sulky, but I couldn't really blame him. Unfortunately, I also didn't have a good answer for him.

We'd moved farther from the hospital, sticking to tunnels and what seemed like abandoned parts of Gardenia. Apparently Ronin had spent the twenty or so minutes we'd been moving thinking of objections to my plan—and reasons why we needed to go immediately into sailor-hunting mode.

I wasn't about to admit I didn't have a plan so I went on the attack. "Hey. You don't have to come."

He sighed. "Look. You're stuck with me. I'll help you with your sister and then, if your lab is the bust I know it'll be, you'll help me run the spacer scam. Deal?"

It wasn't a deal I wanted to make but I wasn't in a great spot for bargaining. "If you can get us out of Gardenia, I can get us the rest of the way to the lab. And if Shena is all right, I'll help you."

Ronin shook his head. "The thing is, I'm running out of time. Whether your sister is okay isn't my problem. I help you, get you out and back in and then you do whatever I want. That's the deal."

"Fine. You get me out and I'll get you some money somehow. But you've got to know that scamming sailors doesn't have any future. Security will be all over us."

"Better Security than Watton."

I hadn't heard that name before but the way Ronin said it made it sound scary. "I said I'd help you."

"Deal." He made it sound like he was doing me a huge favor.

Which reminded me ... "There is one other thing."

He glanced at me, then looked away fast. "No way am I letting you suck my blood."

I wasn't that crazy about the idea either but I didn't want to end up in the middle of nowhere and not have the antibodies I needed. "I won't take much. I bet just a cup or so would probably give me enough—"

"No way. You can suck on the sailors we scam."

I didn't feel that hunger the tri-ds made a big deal over. But Ronin's reading of the medical data-strip had been brutally clear. I'd need blood if I was going to stay healthy.

On the other hand, Ronin obviously wasn't prepared to negotiate on this. Not now, anyway. I'd just have to hope I could last until I found a more agreeable victim.

"We'll try it your way," I said. "Assuming you can get us out of town."

****

Mjolnir had been a mineral-rich moon when it was discovered. Early settlers had mined it so extensively they'd hollowed out huge sections. In the process, they'd created both the deep pit that formed the base of Gardenia's dome, and the need for the major shipping center that Gardenia turned into. With its huge deposits of almost pure water ice, carbon and iron, Mjolnir had attracted prospectors, traders and thieves and Gardenia had become the largest refueling platform this side of Freyja.

When the richest deposits tailed out, the big mining operations moved on but the refining and shipping center were cheaper to create than to move so they were abandoned behind. To get some use out of the now-surplus equipment, freelance prospectors had spread through the system, mining asteroids and sending ore back to Gardenia for processing. The hollowed-out core of Mjolnir was now mostly worthless silicates, calcium and other trash, but a planetoid is big—there were plenty of low-quality mines that made sense to operate given that operators could pick up mining and ore transport equipment for a song.

Where there were mines, there was ore-hauling equipment, and I knew how to use it.

I'd thought my parents were paranoid. From my earliest memory, they'd constantly drilled Shena and me with how to survive any of a thousand lab disasters. I couldn't count the times my mother had me run through the coordinates of the ice mines closest to the lab—and the paths that the robotic ore hoppers took. She'd intended us to use them to get away from the lab to the supposed safety of Gardenia but, using those coordinates and directions in reverse, I could trace my way back to the lab... if

Ronin could get me a skinsuit so my body didn't explode in Mjolnir's near-vacuum and then get both of us past whatever monitors Security had on travel to and from Gardenia.

As far as I could tell, though, he'd been leading me in circles. I swear I saw the same broken-down shop with the same faded 'final sale' e-paper displays three times as he navigated me across Gardenia.

"This way." Ronin gestured toward what looked like a pothole.

I'd been in town a few times, but I never would even have seen the little hole in the highway. I certainly wouldn't have thought to climb into it.

Apparently the road had caved into one of the abandoned mineshafts that honeycombed the planetoid and nobody had bothered fixing it beyond tossing in whatever garbage they had at hand.

Security and the other management corporations were supposed to use their fees to repair the town—for one thing, they had to leak air something fierce. But the corporations had better things to do with their money—like mount raids on labs trying to break their monopolies and kidnap children while they were at it. I didn't think they wanted Gardenia to die, they just didn't want to spend any of their money to save it.

As it was, I suspected in a few years, the road would finish caving in and would dead-end—assuming that Gardenia wasn't abandoned before then. The danger of something going wrong increased as the value of the platform decreased.

Like the corporations, though, I had more pressing concerns to worry about than Gardenia's long-term survival. I had a sister to rescue and every hour that passed made it that much less likely I'd be in time. So, I followed Ronin into the hole and then down another long-abandoned mining tunnel.

The first hundred meters were so narrow I doubted an adult could fit—but two skinny teens had no problem. As we emerged from the mined-out vein, Ronin flashed his laser-cutter, exposing what looked like an old-time cathedral with stone pillars holding up the ceiling ... at least partially, and a crumbled rockfall that served as a stairway down from our tunnel into the main shaft.

"You can turn that out," I said. "There's plenty of light."

"No," he said. "There isn't. It's pitch black in here. But don't worry, I know my way. Just hang onto my pants and I'll lead you."

Holding onto his pants was more personal than I wanted to get. I did follow him and I could see perfectly well. I wondered if Ronin's implants were even worse than mine... and then I remembered that my implants were inactive. So, why could I see in the dark?

The next hundred meters or so were rough—in places, the ice had once descended dozens of meters downward leaving leg-breaking falls. In other places the rocks from above had fallen—and more looked ready to tumble onto our heads.

We passed any number of shafts leading out—most of them looking a lot like the way we'd come in. Then, though, Ronin led me to a much larger access tunnel with laser-cut, glassy walls.

Ronin stopped, turned around, and flashed the laser-cutter too close to my eyes.

"You can see in the dark, can't you?" He sounded mad.

"I thought everyone got the implants."

"If you mean infrared, yeah. Except there is no infrared. It's completely cold here. If you can see, it's vampire sight."

"That's—"

"Cool feature." Ronin looked around, as if someone might actually be listening in this pit. "You think, if you bite me, I'll turn into a vampire, too? A lot of places I go, it'd be useful to see in the dark."

"I'm doubting that biting would change you. If every time someone got bit they turned into a vampire, we'd all be vampires in no time."

He sighed. "I guess that would be too easy."

Oh yeah. Like everything was so easy for me. We were hunched over now—the access tunnel was only a bit over a meter in height—just tall enough that crawling seemed silly but too short to stand upright.

After what seemed like an eternity, we reached a corroded airlock.

"You're kidding," I said when he stopped and punched in an access code. "This piece of junk was an antique when they started

31

mining Mjolnir. And you're telling me it's all that's keeping the atmosphere in Gardenia?"

"The whole platform is falling apart," Ronin said. "Anyone with sense and money has gotten off. Nobody cares about safety since it's just us losers left behind. Every few weeks, something goes wrong—an airlock fails, a meteor penetrates the shield, something goes wrong. And the old, worn-out maintenance bots head down, throw another patch on top of the last bad patch. Every time, there's just a little less resilience, so one day they'll send down the bots and it won't be enough."

"Well," I said. "That's depressing."

"I think it's why Security is so paranoid. They don't want to admit they're losers, too." When the airlock door opened, he grabbed a couple of rebreather-tanks from where they'd been hidden beneath a pile of slag that looked like every other pile of slag and handed me one.

"Poor Security," I said. "I guess their being losers make it okay for them to go around killing people and turning others into vampires."

"They're trying to get all the money out of this rock that they can."

"I guess." I gestured at my makeshift outfit. "I need a skinsuit, too."

"Yeah, I forgot." He reached up into the airlock locker and pulled down an emergency skinsuit, then handed it to me.

"Turn around," I told him.

"So you can jump me? I don't think so."

"Then turn off your cutter. I'm not undressing in front of you."

"Like I'd look at a scrawny vampire."

That sort of hurt but I made him turn around anyway and struggled into the cheap skinsuit.

Fortunately, even cheap skinsuits are nanobe-equipped so they automatically resize to fit whoever wears them. It just took a couple of minutes for it to tighten around my body after I'd put it on although it was big enough it could have fit a giant at first. While it was shrink-wrapping me, I draped the sheet over myself. It was going to be cold out there and the sheet would provide at least some protection. Besides, skinsuits might cover you, but they don't leave a lot to the imagination.

"You can turn around now," I told him as I snapped the rebreather into place.

"You know your sister won't be there, right?" he said. "Security wouldn't be dumb enough to just leave her."

"They were after the Hasro. I was just a bonus."

"Don't count on it. They do what they want, take who they want, and nobody can say anything about it."

All of a sudden, this didn't sound like a generic complaint about how tough it was getting by in the platform. It sounded personal.

"They take someone close to you?"

He turned away. "Seal your mask and let's go."

We stepped into the airlock chamber, sealed the entry hatch behind us and switched on the pumps to evacuate the air back to Gardenia. The airlock groaned. The seals looked abraded—I suspected they leaked a lot. But it still cycled us through.

****

The tunnel looked almost unchanged on the other side of the airlock—glassy rock walls, tunnels diverging off the main trail, and the ever-present dust of the disintegrating moonlet. Although there was no obvious visible difference, my other senses insisted there was one.

A few steps on, I realized I wasn't hearing anything outside my own body and the rebreather.

Well duh. We were in vacuum.

I grabbed Ronin by the arm. "How far," I signed.

He stared at me dumbly.

Oh, yeah. He couldn't see in the darkness.

I shrugged but he didn't see that either.

Finally he got the message I wanted to communicate. He fired up his laser-cutter again, heating a chip of stone until it glowed.

"Never mind," I signed.

He shook his head but led us on.

It couldn't have been more than a kilometer but it seemed like forever before we reached a dead end.

"Straight up," he signed.

33

I hadn't really noticed that the mine had gotten lighter. Now that he'd pointed it out, it was hard to miss.

Thor glowed directly overhead through what had once apparently been an elevator shaft up from an old mine. Unlike Gardenia, where the scratched glass dome dulled the view of Thor, here its beauty was unobscured. The gas giant provided a bit of light despite Mjolnir's lack of atmosphere to scatter the photons.

Once, elevators had carried mining bots down and precious water out this shaft. Now, it was a vertical chimney that climbed, if my depth perception hadn't also been affected by my vampirism, a good hundred meters. Mjolnir's gravity was pretty minimal, but the walls were glassy-slick and the shaft was too wide to straddle.

"How are we supposed to get up that?" Like everyone, I'd learned to sign at the same time as I'd learned to talk. I guess there were people back on Earth who never went into the vacuum, but I wasn't one of them. In space, signing is more important than talking out loud.

Ronin grinned at my question, then pointed into the darkness.

"What?"

Even with my enhanced vision, I could have looked for a year without noticing the monofilament that draped down the shaft like a spiderweb.

The graphene line was thinner than spider silk—only a few molecules thick. It was also far stronger—I suspected it would have supported a ten-thousand kilogram freight of ice. Climbing up wasn't an attractive option, though. If I tried to grab onto it, I'd slice my fingers off more easily than would a doctor's laser-scalpel.

Ronin dragged what looked like a bunch of sticks from beneath another stack of rubble and it finally dawned on me that this wasn't just an escape route he'd stumbled across. This had to be a smuggling tunnel.

I tried not to think about what would happen if the smugglers came across us. My parents had kept my sister and me hidden when smugglers had come to the lab to pick up Hasro, but everyone whispered about how dangerous they could be.

Ronin's sticks glittered in Thor's dull glow and I hazarded a guess. "Diamond?"

"Yeah." Ronin grinned. "I hear diamond used to be worth something."

If so, it had been a long time ago. Admittedly, carbon was the basis for just about all technology, just like hydrogen was the basis for all energy storage. But that didn't make carbon valuable—there was just too much of the stuff and converting from mineral carbon to graphene or diamond was easy enough—I'd often done it in my home lab.

Ronin fired his laser at one of the diamond sticks.

"Hello," I signed. "You can't melt diamond." I knew that from my lab work, too.

"Keep your fingers still and watch."

The laser left a polished clean surface. He dabbed it with something from the tube, then stuck the cleaned facet to the graphene line.

I thought it would melt the line. Instead, it stuck.

Then he did the same thing again a few feet higher.

"The trick when you climb," he explained, "is not to touch the line. Oh, and don't take too long. The epoxies are timed to last for about three minutes but this tube is getting old."

With just one line, climbing looked impossible. The diamond bars would tip if you stepped on either side, and tipping meant cutting my body in half through the monofilament.

"You inch upward," he explained. "Grab the highest diamond you can, pull legs up, balance, then push your back against the wall until you can grab a higher diamond. It isn't easy."

Half an hour later, as I watched the diamond stick I'd just left clatter into the darkness below, I was prepared to admit Ronin had made the understatement of the century.

****

At Earth-gravity, I never would have made it. Even on Mjolnir, I was panting like a mythical Earth-dog by the time we reached the moon's surface. After all, my muscles were adjusted for this gravity. Put me on a one-G planet like old Earth and I'd collapse, vampire enhancement or not.

We sprawled on a slag pile near the elevator shaft. Only when the rebreather caught up with my oxygen demand did I find the energy to stare around, which should have done first thing just in case any smugglers were prowling the neighborhood.

As I'd suspected, the elevator terminated in a former mining area. Smelters and mining bots, most of them missing arms or showing dents in their A.I. housing, were scattered as if someone had planned on returning the following day but had gotten lost on the way back.

There had been a mining dome overhead once, letting any human manager breathe and, of course, get some protection from the electro-magnetic radiation coming from Thor or from Asgard, the distant sun.

Most of the dome remained but it didn't hold any atmosphere in any more. A hole the size of a lifepod had never been repaired.

"So," Ronin signed when we'd finally recovered enough breath to do anything but lie on the ground and pant. "I got us out, as promised. Now you owe me."

"Yeah," I signed back. "I owe you. Now let's go find my sister."

Chapter Four

Mine hoppers are dumb—they're built that way on purpose.

They walk the same route thousands of times, pick up a load of ore, drop it off at the smelter, then do it again… and again. Even a halfway intelligent A.I. would go into a funk if asked to do that. So, hoppers aren't given halfway intelligent A.I.s. Their A.I.s are about as smart as the rocks they haul.

Hoppers need a tiny bit of intelligence to deal with occasional changes in the location of mine outtakes, and they need to be smart enough not to run into each other or fall into holes in the ground. But that's about it.

Since hoppers are programmed to travel the same routes unless they run into obstacles, Ronin and I just had to walk to a mashed-in spot of rock where we spotted hopper tracks and wait.

Sure enough, maybe ten minutes later, a hopper walked by.

We clambered up the sides, punishing muscles I'd already overworked in that ridiculous climb up the mineshaft, and jumped into the hopper chamber which was, naturally, empty for the outgoing journey.

Empty except a few chunks of ice frozen to the supposedly non-stick surfaces—and which dug into my skin while simultaneously freezing me. If Ronin hadn't found me some boots, I would have been in real trouble. You don't lose a lot of heat to the vacuum, but Mjolnir's surface temperature averaged fifty below—Celsius so any touch contact could freeze skin in a fraction of a second.

"What are we going to do on the way back when this thing is loaded?" Ronin asked when we'd settled down.

Our side of Mjolnir always faced Thor, which provided some protection from solar gamma rays but added its own dangers. A couple of inches of reinforced steel from the hopper made a nice additional shield—a shield we wouldn't have when the hopper was full of ice for the return trip.

"We'll figure some ..." a huge yawn chose that moment to grab me. " ...thing out," I finally concluded.

Ronin was looking in my direction and he looked concerned. Once again, I realized that I could see and he couldn't. This vampire thing definitely had some advantages. For one thing, he might not be able to tell if I was awake, which might slow any thought he had about taking advantage of me.

Clearly, though, staying awake indefinitely wasn't one of vampirism's advantages. Despite my best efforts, my eyes blinked shut.

Panic hit me and I forced them open. I couldn't trust anyone, and Ronin was a criminal—a killer either in fact or at least in intent. Even if he couldn't see me, I'd probably snore or something and he'd figure it out. Falling asleep while alone with him was about as stupid as anything I'd ever done.

Stupid or not, I couldn't help myself. Fatigue washed over me like a wave of liquid oxygen, knocking me out as cold as a cryo would.

Wonder if I'll wake up, was my last conscious thought.

****

"Wake up."

I reacted without thought to the attack, twisting with the hand that grasped at my shoulder, controlling my assailant's fist and driving the man behind it into the steel wall.

The lack of a clang reminded me of where I was—in a vacuum. Since I'd heard his voice before, Ronin must have gone helmet to helmet in an attempt to communicate while grabbing me at the same time. Turned out, that hadn't been his smartest strategy.

I opened my eyes in time to see Ronin rubbing his shoulder.

"Sorry," I signed.

He couldn't see me, of course. So I popped open the hopper lid and tried again. "You all right?"

"You don't fight like a girl," he signed. "That a vampire thing?"

"Yeah. If vampires all have … had my father." I didn't think my voice broke, completely. It was close, though. I'd spent thousands of hours with my father, working on the forms, understanding the way joints move … and don't move. And now, he'd never drive me crazy with his constant demands again.

38

"Oh," I rushed on. "Anyway, I think we're at the end of the road. The hopper is just moving a few meters every ten seconds or so." Which had to be why he'd awakened me. Talk about letting him know what he already knew.

If I'd had my implants working, I would have known where we were. As it was, I had to use deduction... something I wasn't used to. "Let's get out of here," I signed. "Before—"

The hopper lurched forward again, its barely opened lid swinging upward.

I blinked against the sudden planet-light from Thor overhead and then saw a tube extending downward toward where the two of us huddled.

"Watch out." Like an idiot, I spoke out loud, which is to say, in the complete silence of vacuum.

At least I didn't stand still, though, as high-pressure liquid water chilled way below freezing poured into the hopper.

I didn't, but Ronin seemed frozen in place—which was exactly what he would be if he didn't move. I realized his eyes might not have adjusted as quickly as mine.

Oh, hell. I grabbed Ronin and dragged him out.

We were both iced by the time I got him out but we hadn't drowned. More to the point, we hadn't frozen—the super-pressurized water turned solid as soon as it hit.

I was happy to have survived the moment until I noticed Ronin looking at me funny. So, I had to check myself out.

Yeah, I was a mess. The hospital sheet I still wore was tough, but eight hours in the hopper had tested its filth-resistance past the breaking point. And the water—well, the thing had been too form-fitting before. Now it made it obvious the cheap skinsuit underneath hadn't been designed to hide anything.

"Pervert," I signed.

He shrugged. "I'm a guy. I can't help looking."

"Maybe. But I bet not all guys would leer."

He shook his head. I noticed his hands were shaking a little when he signed the next words. "Maybe your father wouldn't. A normal guy, though—"

He stopped, probably because he noticed I was sobbing.

"What?"

I tried to catch my breath. This was ridiculous—I needed to act like an adult, not some weepy child. Still, the mention of my father set off the waterworks. "My father. He ... well, he isn't going to leer at anyone ever again ... because he's dead. And Security killed him."

"Oh." Ronin's hands dropped to his side. He didn't know what to say next and neither did I. I mean, you know your parents aren't going to live forever. They were really old—my father was almost forty and my mother not much younger. And they'd been annoying—my mother with her constant testing us on emergency procedures and my father with me never being good enough in kung fu no matter how much I studied. But still, I couldn't imagine going through the rest of my life without them.

"Come on," I signed. "These rebreathers aren't going to last forever."

Ronin seemed happy to be let off the hook. A part of me needed to talk about it, work through what it meant to be an orphan and responsible for my sister. But I couldn't just dump that on him and even if I could, I didn't know what I would say. I mean, yeah, I was sad that my parents were gone. And yeah, I felt bad because I'd rolled my eyes when mom had made us practice the emergency evacuation procedures that were getting me back to the lab right now. And maybe even, yeah, I should have been at the controls when Security had attacked. Not that I could have done anything, but at least I would have died with the others.

I blinked away my tears. All I needed was to freeze my eyes shut ... or open for that matter.

"I gotta orient myself." I used that as an excuse to look out, taking in Thor, the fixed stars, and the other planets.

One nice thing about no atmosphere—the stars are always there.

"Got it." I tugged on Ronin's arm. "Follow me."

He rubbed his shoulder again and I noticed a dark patch in his skinsuit. He must have hit that rough hopper wall harder than I'd thought when I'd imagined he was attacking. And the dark stain ... that had to be ... blood.

****

I'd seen ancient tri-ds set on old Earth. In the oldest of them, people ate animal flesh and didn't even think about it. Not the processed blue-green algae we called 'meat' but actual animals they had slaughtered and carved up. Just thinking of it had always creeped me out—along with everyone else I knew. Not that anyone on Earth ate meat any more—as far as anyone knew people on Earth didn't eat much at all, which was why their fleets raided space colonies—for food.

Any more, nobody cut up any animal more complex than a multicellular yeast and even if they did, they wouldn't eat them. Partly it was religious. Partly it was economic—growing animals for food is a huge waste of resources. Either way, it wasn't going to happen. So, if I wouldn't eat cows or chickens, the idea of biting into people and sucking their blood was even more disgusting. Or it should be.

I couldn't help staring at that bloody stain on Ronin's skinsuit, though. And the more I looked, the more my mouth watered. Yes, I knew it was disgusting. Still, some part of me wanted to suck down human blood.

I must have been staring at him ten times as hard as he'd stared at my wet sheet because Ronin finally noticed.

His hand went back to his shoulder, this time covering it up. "Oh, no," he signed. "Not happening."

"I don't really want your blood," I signed. "I mean, I can't imagine actually biting into your flesh, feeling for a vein just filled with rich warm blood and sucking it dry."

Except talking about it made me think about it, made me imagine it in vivid detail. The whole idea was still disgusting ... but it also had an appeal I couldn't deny. What I also couldn't deny was that I was shaky. Even in Mjolnir's light gravity, my knees wanted to wobble.

Still, I wasn't going to attack him and take his blood. Although, maybe I should, I thought. After all, someone had to stop him from killing sailors and getting Security after all of us. It would be justified, even—

I nipped that thought hard, before it got too convincing. "Come on," I signed.

If we were moving, I wouldn't have to look at that flowing blood, wouldn't have to think about running my tongue over his battered skin and sucking in—

I walked straight into a barely moving hopper. Yeah, just maybe I was way too distracted.

From there, I put all of my concentration into putting one foot in front of the next, into watching out for holes in the ground, into avoiding the hoppers and mining bots that scrambled across the landscape of this working mine. Into anything other than my desire for blood.

Hours of sleep in the hopper should have restored my strength, but I felt weak, almost lightheaded as we walked. Moving in very light gravity isn't as easy it sounds. It doesn't take a lot of muscle to lift off the ground, but it's still easy to break a leg when you come down and it takes concentration not to slip into holes and twist something. Still, it shouldn't have been that hard ... and Ronin shouldn't have kept distracting me with his blood.

***

My parents' old lab blended with the environment. Partly, that was intentional. If you're producing drugs that compete with Security's self-proclaimed monopoly, you don't want to call attention to yourself. Partly it was because just about everything built on Mjolnir was constructed out of the rocks left over when the water and iron were mined out. And partly because every bit of Mjolnir was littered with abandoned structures, abandoned hopes of those who had thought to make their fortunes in what had once been the most active shipping channel between Earth's first-generation colonies and the newer third generation settlements.

My mother, in what I'd always considered her paranoid fantasies, had dragged Shena and me out of the lab in rebreathers, taking us on long hikes to a dozen possible escape sites—one of which was the water mine where Ronin and I had landed. So, I'd been this way before. I was still relieved when the landmarks my mother had drilled into my brain finally started showing up. If I'd gotten turned around and went in the wrong direction, I didn't know if I could make it back.

I slowed when we approached one of the lab's emergency exits—one that didn't appear to be violated—then tensed as Ronin got closer. I couldn't smell the blood in the vacuum of space but I knew it was there.

He stopped before he touched me, possibly remembering what had happened the last time he'd grabbed me without warning. I didn't need a boyfriend, and if I did any boyfriend I would take wouldn't be a criminal. That still didn't mean I wanted the only guy around to be so afraid of me he didn't even dare get near me.

"What?" I signed.

He gestured off to our right.

I'd been so focused on the little signs and hints I'd memorized that that I'd missed the huge hole. Security hadn't just infected the lab with their vampire virus, they'd blown it up after they'd finished.

"You still think your sister is here?" he signed.

One good thing about signing. It gives you time to think before you say something like "stick it where Asgard doesn't shine." Instead I signed, "I'll check."

With the lab open to the vacuum, the chances Shena had survived were low. But I'd left her in the atmosphere filtration system which, in turn, was connected directly to the oxygen generation plant. If there was anywhere a kid could hide and live, it was there.

The lab had never been anything beyond marginally functional. Bare stone walls extruded from mine tailings had held in most of the atmosphere and kept out most of Asgard's radiation. Carbon-steel fermentation vessels had connected to silica-glass distillation tanks that used the pressure differential between the lab's pressurized interior and the vacuum outside to boil off volatiles, cutting down on energy use and making the lab less visible to Security's infrared detection. Or so we'd thought. Security had found it anyway.

Security's explosives had reduced the lab's usual controlled chaos to a collection of shards—glittering glass, gleaming steel, and dull rock.

Here and there, lumps stood a little taller than the rest of the rubble.

I thought at first that these might be bigger hunks of wall. Closer inspection proved otherwise. Security hadn't bothered cleaning up the lab... or the victims of their attack.

The sight was enough to make Ronin forget the way I'd directed him into the hopper wall ... and the way I'd stared at that bloodstain on his shoulder. He grabbed me, his fingers signing so fast they stuttered. "Jeez. Y-y-you got dead people everywhere."

And this was the guy I was supposed to count on to sneak up behind sailors and mug them?

I'd thought I was out of tears but I'd been wrong. I shook my head under the rebreather and nodded.

Still, I wasn't here for them, I was here for my sister. "Help me count them."

"That's morbid."

"Gotta be done."

There had been eight of us on the station. My parents were two. Captain Russart and his slimy assistant Bert Harding were four. Dr. Bently and Daniella Porter were six. My sister and I filled out the quota.

I was still alive, so there should be seven bodies.

We found five and identified them. My mother was in the cryo where I'd left her but the machine was powered off and her body left exposed to vacuum. My father's body hung off of a chair in front of the lab controls. It looked like he'd been trying to deal with the lab emergencies when the poison gas had gotten him.

Shena and Harding were missing.

I'd never liked Harding—the way he looked at me and my sister made my spine shiver and not in a good way. Still, I'd be forever grateful if he'd spirited her away during the attack.

I tried to remember where Harding had been when the lab had been breached but my failed implant meant I couldn't just replay the last moments of the lab's existence.

I could hope Harding had rescued Shena but I hadn't come all this way just to assume she was being taken care of. There could be two more bodies somewhere else in the lab, including inside the atmosphere scrubber where I'd left Shena.

The air filtration system was located off to the side of the lab, carved into the living stone of Mjolnir to reduce the chance of accidental damage from settling mineshafts or space debris. There wasn't anything accidental about a Security raid, but the solid bedrock figured to stand up to the explosives better than anything extruded. Despite everything, it wasn't completely impossible that we'd find Shena there, alive and waiting for me.

I checked each duct as I passed it.

None was outgassing. Which could mean the filtration system fail-safes had actually sensed the vacuum and sealed the filtration system the way they were supposed to. Or it could mean that Security had sabotaged the fail-safes there as well.

Considering the amount of destruction I saw everywhere, I didn't think Security would just leave a perfectly functional oxygen generation system for the next band of criminals who wanted to set up another unlicensed lab. Still, couldn't be positive and I wasn't going to stop looking for Shena until I found her ... or her body.

Ronin followed me as I punched the manual access code into the filtration system's maintenance hatchway.

Nothing happened.

"Obviously they destroyed it," he signed.

I teared up like a little girl and took out my frustration on him. "So, get me a steel bar or something. I'm going in."

Instead he found a power ram, its fuel cell apparently still full of hydrogen.

Showing more intelligence than I expected, or maybe just because his hands were full of power tool, Ronin refrained from saying anything, instead simply attacking the hinges that held the hatch in place.

My fingers itched to tell him to be careful—if the oxygen generator was working, that hatch door would shoot off like a cannon from differential pressure.

Then I noticed that he was already staying clear. I wasn't the only person who paid attention to what was going on.

When he finally got it loosened, the door dropped straight down—with no puff of cooling gas.

My heart dropped as quickly as the hatch. If Shena had followed my instructions and stayed put, she was dead.

I didn't want to look. Which was idiotic. Shena wasn't Schrodinger's cat, halfway alive until someone saw her dead. I couldn't help her by prolonging my uncertainty, and I still had the long shot that maybe Harding had taken her with him on his escape.

While I dithered, Ronin climbed through the hatch and used the ram to peel off countless layers of activated graphene filters.

"Nobody here," he signed. "But there is one thing." He pointed to a man-sized hole in the side wall. "Somebody came in without learning the access codes."

The wreckage didn't show signs of explosive decompression, which meant that somebody, presumably Security, had broken through before they'd destroyed the rest of the lab. If Shena had waited where I'd told her, they would have found her.

Maybe they'd killed her. Maybe she was still alive. Until I found her body, I'd keep looking.

Security wasn't in the charity business. If they'd captured her, I couldn't just show up at headquarters, give them an atta-boy and sign her out. Instead, they'd have her bundled off toward some richer system where slave merchants would snap up a cute eleven-year-old as fast as a black hole sucks in hydrogen. So, if she was alive and they had her, she might be out of my reach.

Rather than think about that, I spent ten minutes filtering through the graphene, making absolutely sure she wasn't hidden in some corner. Finally, I convinced myself of the truth. Shena was gone. Since Security had left the corpses behind, she'd probably been taken alive. Just as I had. Since Harding knew the hatch codes, it was probably Security who'd taken her. Unless he'd gotten to her first and they'd just made the holes to make the lab harder to resettle.

"We've got to get her back," I told Ronin.

He shook his head. "Not happening. I kept my part of the deal. Now you help me roll sailors. I need money—bad."

Even if I'd been willing to attack innocent sailors, I didn't see how that would help Shena.

"Want to tell me why you need money so bad?"

"Everyone needs money."

"Not so much that they'd commit suicide by Security. You know that rolling sailors is a losing game. Security will come down on you so hard you'll be bouncing in low-grav. And killing sailors instead of just robbing them might slow Security a bit at first but it'll make them a lot more angry, and a lot more determined to find you."

Ronin looked away. "I've racked up some debt, okay?" he muttered. "I'd rather have Security after me than Watton."

"What's a Watton?"

"A crime boss. Watton is his name and I think he's human although people like to argue that point. I owe him thousands."

The more I'd thought about it, the more I'd realized my initial reaction had been right—I'd be crazy to follow Ronin's plan. But if Security had Shena, I'd need help to get her free. A crime boss might know the levers to pull and I could use someone, even if it was just Ronin, watching my back.

"Suppose I can help you with the money thing," I said. "Without killing sailors. I do that, will you keep helping me with my sister?"

He stared at me. Even the rebreather mask didn't hide his skepticism.

"You help *me* with the money? You couldn't even buy yourself a pair of boots."

"That reminds me, I need to get a real skinsuit instead of this piece of junk while we're here. First things first, though. Do we have a deal?"

"You pay off what I owe, you can ask me to do just about anything. Because Watton is tired of waiting and I figure he'll make an example out of me about five minutes after he finds me. And there's no place in Gardenia I can hide."

"Okay, then there's one thing we need to do before we head back."

Captain Russart had been paranoid but he hadn't been as good at it as my mother. The air ducts in the lab were so small even the tiniest child would get stuck in the first turn—I knew because years before when I'd first started exploring I'd barely made it out after a hairy half-hour trapped. But, where a person couldn't go, though, a camera-bot had no trouble.

I led Ronin to the captain's cabin.

Russart's cache blended perfectly with the stone floor... once we moved his body off of it. So perfectly I didn't think Security would have found it.

And they hadn't.

There wasn't any cash, of course. Anyone trying to use physical money might as well put a sign on their forehead asking for Security to check them. What there was was Hasro. Lots of it. The captain wasn't a private entrepreneur. He'd been making Hasro for businesses somewhere in Gardenia—for people who could pay off Security, handle distribution, and pocket most of the money. Like many of the underworld, Russart wasn't completely honest in his dealings with his supposed bosses. He'd skimmed off a good chunk of the hasro. He'd probably had some scheme for dealing with Gardenia's criminal class and keeping the money for himself.

"Interesting," Ronin signed when I'd opened the cache and dragged out vacuum-pack after vacuum-pack of pure dope.

He weighed one of the packs with his hand and then counted the remainder. "We can do something with this."

"What we can do is find my sister." I made Ronin carry the Hasro out while I took another look at Captain Russart.

His blood was mostly dry but ...

I felt sick to my stomach but much stronger when I rejoined Ronin a couple of minutes later.

Chapter Five

The oxygen rebreather had practically become part of me by the time we made it back to Gardenia and dumped it next to the airlock.

When we left the rebreathers, Ronin insisted on replacing the used chemicals with fresh batches we'd picked up at the lab, removing the exhausted cartridges for reconditioning.

I spent that time breathing through my nose. I would have thought that thirty hours in vacuum would leave me clean. After all, it's supposed to be bacteria that make people stink and the combination of vacuum and high-frequency electromagnetic waves are supposed to kill bacteria.

Apparently, whatever stink-makers attached to us had skipped that science lesson. Ronin and I reeked like week-old sewage.

When we made it back to Gardenia, I made Ronin spring for sonic cleansing at a public bathhouse for both of us. We needed to deal and nobody would deal with someone who stunk so bad.

Once our stink quotient was under control, we stashed our drugs and headed for the underworld.

I'd been afraid to bring Ronin in on the Hasro. He was a petty crook, had befriended me only in exchange for my promise to help him in an insane scam that would certainly leave me the obvious target for Security. But he'd had plenty of chances to hurt me and instead had kept his bargain. Besides, he knew the Gardenia underworld—even if that meant he owed it a lot of money.

By Security's standards I was a far more dangerous criminal than Ronin—I'd helped with Russart's drug production and I'd gone vampire. But that didn't mean I knew my way around the Gardenia underworld. If I tried to deal the Hasro myself, I was far more likely to run into a Security sting than I was to find someone who could move the quantity we'd liberated from Russart's cache. Considering what had happened at Russart's lab, I didn't even have to guess what Security would do if they caught me trying to break their monopoly.

Ronin didn't travel in crime's upper circles either, but the guy he owed all the money to did—so we had a chance to pay off Ronin's cash problem with enough left over to let me find Shena. Plus, if I paid off Ronin's debt and saved his life, instead of me owing Ronin, he'd owe me. I'd feel a lot more comfortable with that.

I followed Ronin to one of the sailor bars near the docks hoping he wasn't going to suddenly revert to his earlier plan.

Apparently a ship called Wren-Earth had recently docked, spilling its sailors and their money into Gardenia. Naturally Gardenia's residents worked every angle to make sure none of that money went back to the ship. With the sailors trying to make up for months in space, I suspected they'd succeed.

The first thing I noticed when we walked in was the line of sailors leaning against the bar. A few of them wore sailor whites but most had on garish clothes garnished with bling reflecting all the ports they'd visited.

A couple of local women and a boy younger than Shena were already hustling, their dilated pupils promising that they'd feel no pain no matter what the sailors did to them. Another girl slipped in behind us and immediately went to the bar to rub up against a sailor.

On the stage, a woman danced to the beat of music only those who paid for it could hear. As I watched, she shed her top, showing pale skin, bony ribs, and a smile that even a sailor on a male-only ship would have to guzzle a dozen drinks to believe in.

I'd seen plenty of sailor bars in the tri-ds. If this place was typical, the tri-ds got the hard-drinking and hard-fighting part right, but I'd never seen a video that captured the hopeless dull faces, the stink of decades of spilled beer, neo-opium, Hasro and synth-whiskey, or the high-pitched shrieks and artificial levity of girls and boys intent on taking the sailors' money no matter how painful or humiliating the process might be.

Ronin led me over to a table manned by a dirty teen and jerked his thumb at the kid. "Tell Watton I've got an offer for him."

"You ain't my boss."

"Carsley, you won't have a boss if Watton learns you wouldn't let me see him and I had to go to Barkley with my deal."

50

"Yeah?" Carsley flicked a mono-steel open, then shut. "I'll tell him. And if he gives me grief for bothering him, I'll give you ten times as much." He stared at me, then ran his tongue over his teeth. "Oh, and I'll own your femm."

"Hey," I put in. "Nobody—"

"I told you," Ronin pretended I hadn't said anything, "Watton will want this."

Carsley leered obviously at me while he slowly finished his beer. He glanced toward the bar as if considering buying another but instead got up and sauntered toward the bathroom.

"Your big criminal lives in the toilet?" I signed.

"You're hiring me to help you," Ronin fired back. "So, let me do my job."

I was okay with that but I wasn't comfortable with the feel of the crowd. The sailors recognized the drugged-up women and children for what they were... versions of what they could find in every port. Ronin and I were different and they were curious about us. Maybe I shouldn't have insisted on the sonic shower after all.

A waitress wandered our way. Her top lacked any obvious fasteners and perpetually seemed at the point of gaping open to reveal all beneath it without ever quite doing so. I made a note to figure out how to do that— not that I had much of a chest yet, but you never know.

"You come into the bar," she explained, "you gotta order. You working the sailors, the house gets ten percent of the take... and don't try to cheat." She shuddered. "Believe me, that is a very bad idea."

"We're at Watton's table," Ronin explained. "We've got a business proposition for him."

She shook her head. "Come on, kids. You don't want to piss your lives away. You've got—"

A raspy voice interrupted. "Let's just see what they've got."

The waitress jumped like she'd been hit by a tesla coil and hurried back to the bar.

The speaker had to weigh a hundred-fifty kilos and tower close to two meters. Carsley trailed behind him like a vulture behind a bear.

I suspected we'd rousted the mysterious Watton from his potty lair.

The giant glared at Ronin, then at me. "She's young and pretty, but young and pretty is a drug on the market in Gardenia." He licked his lips. "Still, I like your spirit. Tell you what, I'll take her for half what you owe me. And I'll give you two months at ten percent per week to come up with the rest."

Ronin must be figuring me out because he clamped his hand on my thigh before I got out word one. "I can do a better deal if you—"

A couple of sailors hadn't gotten the message that this was a private meeting.

One of them was almost as big as Watton but all muscle where Watton looked to be mostly fat. He gave Carlsey an elbow and growled at Watton. "Back off, fats. Me and my mates seen the chickens first."

Watton turned up his lips and showed his teeth. I thought he was attempting a smile but it made him look more like a picture I'd once seen of a Centaurian shark than a friendly person. "If you wait a bit, I may be able to give them to you at a discount."

"That's the thing." The sailor shook his head sadly and, to me at least, threateningly. "Me and my mates, we don't like to wait and we don't like sloppy seconds. So, maybe you just get out of our faces, we'll let you have the left-overs."

"Pity." Watton made what looked like a brushing motion and the sailor hurled backward, smashing his head into the bar with a sick crack.

Blood gushed from the man's nose in three spurts, then the gushing stopped … as did his breathing.

"You …" one of the other sailors sputtered for the words. "You killed him."

Watton reached into his tunic and removed a heavy-duty laser-cutter which he placed on the table in front of him. The bartender, slapping a wooden club against his oversized hand, and another man who I assumed was the bar's bouncer, appeared at Watton's side.

"Any trouble, Mr. Watton?" the bartender asked.

"Hey," the sailor whined. "Why you taking his side?"

The bartender swung around hard, leading with his club and the second sailor went down. "Anyone else have complaints about the service?"

I should have been scared stiff by the violence and by the casual way Watton and his assistants handled trouble. I'd known we were dealing with criminals but I hadn't really thought through what that meant ... or what our chances were of actually getting any money out of Watton once we'd delivered the Hasro. Still, a part of me found the dead sailor's blood fascinating, almost compelling.

I pulled myself together when I noticed Watton's gaze on me. When he saw I was paying attention to him again, he deliberately ran his tongue over his lips.

What was it about men and their crude gestures?

"Now," he said after a few seconds of silence. "You say you have a better proposal. Normally I'm not looking to bargain but your good faith in bringing me the little girl speaks well of you."

Ronin handled the negotiation, but Watton's attention was all on me.

After Ronin had told him about our Hasro stash Watton shook his head. "You have twenty kilograms? Uncut? That seems difficult to believe. How could Security have missed such a substantial stash?"

I'd been asking myself the same question. Security hadn't stumbled over the lab. They'd sent in their attack virus and followed it with military precision. Which meant they knew exactly what they were after. Almost as if they had someone inside. Which was the clue I needed. All of a sudden, the other missing body wasn't a mystery any more. It was part of the equation.

"We all knew Bert Harding was a slug," I said. "Although he was Russart's assistant, even Russart wouldn't have been dumb enough to trust him ... or careless enough to let Harding know he didn't. Harding sold out the lab, but he could only tell Security what he knew."

Watton nodded slowly. "Possible. And now you wish to offer the drugs to me. I deal in humans, little miss. Not in drugs. *You* have value to me. If I try to expand into other lines of business, I get Security … and other entrepreneurs … breathing down my neck. Frankly, I don't need that aggravation."

"You know the people who can move quantity." Ronin was trying to get the negotiation back on track. "There's enough at stake here for everyone to get a piece."

"Yet," Watton grasped Ronin around the throat, his hands moving so quickly the younger man didn't even react until his windpipe was being crushed. "And yet," Watton continued as if carrying on a simple conversation, "why should I share? When I can just take it all for myself."

"Two reasons." I hadn't been completely prepared but I'd known something like this would happen. "First, if word gets around that you kill the golden goose, nobody will want to deal with you. And second, we equipped the package with a timed explosive. If we don't enter the code every thirty minutes, there won't be any Hasro for anyone."

Watton shook his head. "Tell me where it's hidden and give me the code or your friend dies."

Although the bar was dark, my enhanced eyesight let me clearly see the purple in Ronin's face.

I made myself shrug. "I give you what you want, you kill him and me and take the drugs. I refuse, you kill him and me and you don't get the drugs. Remind me what's the upside in giving in."

Watton's face twisted. For a second, I thought he would snap Ronin's neck just out of frustration or to call my bluff. Then he laughed, pushed Ronin down on his chair and made a sign at the bartender.

"You know, little girl. I like you. Let's drink to a new partnership."

"Yeah, sure."

I didn't know what to expect until the bartender put two shot-glasses on the table.

From the smell, a lot became perfectly clear. Because Watton had just served up two cups of blood.

Chapter Six

Cut for street use, twenty kilos of pure hasro would sell for millions. We didn't get five percent of that.

With what we did get, we paid off Ronin's debt and got fifty thousand more out of the deal. The good news was that we were alive. As a bonus, Watton promised to get us some info on Harding.

Considering the alternatives, I thought we'd done great. Ronin, not so much.

"We should have gotten at least ten percent of the value." Ronin was signing again. Not because we were back in vacuum, but because Watton had nearly crushed his throat and it hurt him to talk.

"We paid off what you owed," I reminded him. "So, you don't have to risk your life trying to roll sailors who'd just as soon murder you as play your games."

"But he still cheated us."

"He also gave us the contacts we need."

It had cost a good chunk of our fifty thousand, but I'd bought upgraded implants for both Ronin and myself. I never wanted to get caught without the ability to communicate again, so I went with the military option—which allows a manual reboot in case of problems. I was certain it was overkill, but if I'd been asked, I'd have bet it was impossible to shut down an implant the way Security had shut mine down earlier.

I was still getting used to the implant—complete with a new address code that nobody knew—when the message came in.

"Watton?" Ronin asked when he saw my far-away gaze.

"Nobody else knows my address."

Watton's message was brief but important. He had located Harding.

"That's got to be worth a lot," I said. "To me, anyway."

Ronin stared at me for a few seconds, shaking his head when I told him where Harding had ended up. "Watton," he finally said, "set us up to get killed. Maybe he figures he can get his money back when Security kills us."

I didn't think Watton would cry if anything happened to us. Still, I didn't think he'd set us up just to get his money back. For one thing, if somebody killed us, I doubted they'd share whatever loot they found. It didn't matter whether he wanted it that way, though. Barging into Security HQ, where he said Harding was located, would kill us for sure.

***

Gardenia's Security HQ was a grimy stone structure that went so high it actually brushed up against the city's dome.

Much though I wanted to find my sister and much though I felt the time ticking away, I wasn't going into that building. Instead, Ronin and I parked ourselves in a decrepit coffee shop nearby, bought something advertised as 'hot chocolate' although it wasn't especially hot and didn't taste anything like chocolate, and sipped on our cups while we waited to see what happened.

I'd never really thought about Security being at the center of activity, but a constant stream of people—some in uniform, most not—made their way in and out of the building.

I almost didn't recognize Bert Harding when he tagged onto a crowd disgorged from one of Security's elevators and headed for the road. For one thing, he wore the uniform of a Security officer. For another, he'd always worn his hair slicked down with a thick dose of some kind of grease and cringed around the lab like he was afraid of being hit. Now, his hair was frizzy and he walked with authority.

"He's a captain," Ronin reported when I pointed Harding out to him. "This has to be mistaken identity."

I shook my head. "It's Harding. And think about it this way—if he was just some flunkie, once they captured Shena, he'd be out of the loop. A captain is more likely to know where they sent her. I'm going after him."

I abandoned my stone-cold chocolate and headed for the door. "Stay well back from me," I signed. "But keep in sight. We may have to trade off so he won't get suspicious."

Tracking Harding was difficult. The word "suspicious" didn't begin to explain his behavior. He stopped, turned around, doubled back in directions he'd just come from, popped into shops and ducked behind transports. If I'd been alone, he would have spotted me in the first couple of minutes. But Ronin was watching for my signals and we'd both brought a couple of clothing changes so we traded off, walking past when Harding changed direction, going ahead when I thought I knew where he was heading, messaging each other when Harding went on unexpected detours.

I'd never thought of myself as particularly sheltered, but Ronin had shown me a side of Gardenia my parents never have let me visit. We followed Harding to another district I'd never seen—but for a different reason.

Everyone on Mjolnir knew about "The Hill." There, on a piece of the moon that had never been mined, the rich rubbed elbows with each other. From what I'd heard, most of them never even left their enclave.

If my nightmares were right and Shena had been captured to be sold into slavery, this was the kind of neighborhood where she might end up. Assuming she hadn't already left Mjolnir.

Just for a moment, I entertained the fantasy that Harding might have rescued Shena. If he had the kind of money to live in a place like this, surely he could afford to save a girl from the slavers.

Unfortunately, logic forced me to abandon that hope. An undercover Security officer was in the business of destroying his so-called friends. Why would he feel guilty about selling a little girl into slavery?

Still, that didn't mean he wouldn't know where she'd gone. I had to believe he'd know something: it was my only chance.

Even though we'd switched to our best outfits, we weren't dressed well enough for The Hill. Still, we were kids—I gambled that kids from The Hill could be slobs, too.

Ronin and I stepped into an old-fashioned malt shop about five minutes apart. Each of us grabbed a separate table.

A waiter-bot in the form of a pretty waitress about my age trundled over and took my order. I almost fainted from the price, but the whole purpose of getting the money had been to rescue my sister and we needed a spot where we could wait Harding out. This looked like our best bet.

"What if he's in for the night?" Ronin signed under his table where nobody else could see. At least I hoped there wasn't a Security A.I. camera hiding down there.

I shrugged. I didn't know Harding well, but it figured that a Security officer who went undercover for months at a time wouldn't keep a lot of groceries or a mate back home. If I could believe the tri-ds at all, a rich guy would head down to a restaurant to get natural food rather than something he could dial up on his constructor.

Fortunately, Harding lived up to the stereotype. Half an hour after he'd entered his access-controlled building, he came back out.

Again, it took me a second to recognize him. He'd changed from his Security uniform to a standard civilian cover-all and his hair had a different look, somewhat closer to how he'd been in the lab but without the grease.

He headed for a little hole-in-the-wall cookery down the street, grabbed an outside table and ordered something.

I dumped what was left of my malt and headed after him.

Once I was near, I shuffled the rest of the way toward him. "Please, sir. I'm hungry."

He didn't even raise his eyes. "Blow."

"Mr. Harding?" I'd practiced acting surprised with Ronin. Apparently I had a tendency toward over-acting and I needed to get this just right.

"I'm afraid you've got the wrong..." he finally did look up. "Kari Lorne? I thought you were..."

Dead? Vampire? Enslaved?

I'd thought about it a lot before I'd approached him. Finally, I'd decided that the hospital would cover up my disappearance rather than admit they'd let a vampire walk away from their care. Up until now, that was just a guess. If he called his friends in Security, I'd know I guessed wrong.

I watched him carefully, searching for any of the tells that indicate someone has made a phone connection. I didn't see anything but that didn't mean a lot. Harding had fooled everyone in the lab for months—he was an actor.

Keeping quiet would just make it easy for him. Instead, I put on the teenage girl act and gushed. "I've been so worried. I woke up in a hospital here in Gardenia and I've been trying to call my parents ever since but they don't answer. And I've been afraid to call anyone else. What happened? One minute I was working the external monitors in the lab, the next some rude clerk-bots were shoving me out of the hospital because I couldn't pay my bills."

"They let you go?"

I'd dressed younger than I was because I'd wanted Harding to see me as a potential asset, as someone he could bundle off to wherever they'd sent my sister. I pulled a sad face and tried to look pathetic. "Let me go? Ha. They pushed me out."

"Interesting."

"I'm so glad I found you," I rushed on. "With no one from the lab answering my calls, I didn't know what to do. Do you know where my parents are? What about Shena?"

"Ah…"

I watched him closely wondering if I'd see some hint of guilt. I mean, he'd basically killed a half-dozen people he'd worked with, pretended to be friends with. What I saw instead looked like greed.

"I'm sorry to say that your parents didn't make it, Kari."

"What?" I'd thought I would have to manufacture surprise but there was nothing artificial about the grief that hit me. I'd known they were dead, seen their bodies. Still, every time I heard it, it was as if I learned it again.

"I was, ah, doing exterior maintenance when Security hit." He looked so sincere I would have fallen for it if I hadn't seen him in his Security uniform. "You know we were taking a chance making Hasro without paying Security's license fee, but I guess none of us knew how terrible the consequences would be. They killed every single adult who was still inside."

"But…" Calling up tears wasn't any effort at all.

"Because Shena was orphaned, she has been put up for … ah … adoption," he continued.

I hadn't been dumb enough to fall for that one even before the raid. Babies are adopted. Twelve-year-old girls were sold. As were fifteen-year-old girls although, from what I'd heard, we didn't command as high a price as the younger ones did. Admitting I knew that wouldn't be smart so I played dumb for Harding's benefit.

"Nobody needs to adopt her," I said. "She's got family. I'll take care of her. I'll get a job somewhere in Gardenia and we can be together."

"Well ..." He faked careful consideration. "You're underage yourself and if you remember, you were panhandling just now."

"I'm old enough," I said. "I worked at the lab. With your recommendation, I bet I could get a job that would pay plenty."

"That's true," he lied. "Still, it might be better if the two of you could find a foster family together."

"Nobody could replace my parents."

"Of course not." He looked sympathetic. "Nobody would expect you to forget your birth parents. But there are plenty of people who desperately want children of their own but, for whatever reason, are unable to have them."

I supposed that could be true but it didn't sound likely. Anyone rich enough to have children was rich enough for an implant that could cure any infertility problems—and probably rich enough for an incubator to handle the whole pregnancy thing if they'd spent too much time in hard radiation or just didn't want the bother.

"But—"

"You're both attractive children," Harding interrupted, barely managing not to smirk. "I'm absolutely certain there are plenty of ... ah ... foster parents who'd be happy to add both of you to their... families. That way you could be together and ... ah ... pursue your education."

I had a pretty good idea what kind of "education" he had in mind.

"Maybe." I put on a sad face. "But how would I even find her? I mean, once they go into Security ..." I let my voice trail off with some judicious and practiced chin-trembling. Again, the act wasn't hard because I really was worried sick about Shena and I really did fear that she'd be lost in Security's databases, inaccessible to anyone who wasn't cleared for access.

"I had a ... ah ... friend in Security." He tried out a shark-toothed grin. "Maybe I can help you."

"Really? That would be so great, Mr. Harding."

Throwing my arms around him and hugging him was probably the hardest thing I'd ever done. Almost certainly this man had released the virus that had killed my parents and turned me into a vampire. The urge to slide a cutter across his throat and suck out his blood was practically irresistible. I kept reminding myself that he was the key to Shena.

Confirming the worst of my suspicions, he turned slightly as I hugged him, making my practically nonexistent chest rub against him. What a pervert.

When I tugged away from the hug, he grabbed my arm and slid on a plastic cuff.

"What the—"

"Really, Kari. Nobody is that dumb."

"But ... but you're—"

"Security isn't a non-profit. I spent better than a month working Russart's ridiculous operation and for what? My promotion was based on turning in at least two children to Security's child employment services. When those do-gooders in the hospital let you out, they robbed me of what I earned. Now, I'm getting it back."

"You ... you mean you were the one who ..."

"The one who flushed out an unlicensed Hasro lab? Russart thought he was so clever paying off some corrupt Security flunkies to look the other way. The Corporation just isn't that easy to fool—and it's people like Russart who keep me working. I was doing my job when I disabled the sensors so there would be no warning that Security was coming. And I'll be doing my job taking you in." He tried a phony-looking grin. "Who knows, you might end up with your sister after all."

Chapter Seven

Every place has its perverts. Gardenia was no different. Sadly for Security, not enough of Gardenia's perverts were rich enough to buy all of the young girls Security rounded up.

I wasn't surprised that Harding had put the snatch on me. Letting him do exactly that had been the only way I'd been able to figure I could sucker him into putting me together with my sister. But I'd hoped Shena was still somewhere in Gardenia—and that I'd be able to communicate with Ronin for an escape. A slave ship, one already undocked and in orbit, hadn't been on my agenda.

But when they slammed the steel-barred gates of the ship's slave pit behind me, I realized my agenda didn't have a lot to do with reality. Again.

At least I'd been right about the hospital. They couldn't have reported that they'd misplaced a vampire or I'd be dead instead of here.

The fifteen by fifteen meter cell held at least twenty girls, ranging in age from maybe seven to me, a very young-looking fifteen. All of us were filthy. Some had tears in their skintights and might as well have been naked. Several kept their arms wrapped around their scrawny chests, as if that would stop the sailors from taking advantage. Some huddled in fetal positions on the floor either motionless or jerking spasmodically.

The stink hit me like a punch. It wasn't just the smell of *these* girls ... although some of them looked like they'd been locked up for months. The odors of sweat, feces and urine clashing with harsh disinfectants had to have built up over the decades if not centuries.

In the corner of the large cell, a couple of sonic showerheads showed that any cleaning would be on public display. The stainless steel toilet was equally exposed.

I looked around, taking in the conditions, checking to see how the steel bars were welded into the floor, seeking something that would give me a chance to get out of this mess.

Maybe, I thought, *the crew got their kicks out of watching filthy young girls taking care of their hygiene needs.* If so, they'd surely seen more than they could stand by now. Because this slave ship was old ... so old that they'd used steel, rather than stronger and lighter graphene, to build the cells and bars that locked us in. There had to be some turnover among the crew but even so, I had to hope that anyone on guard would have become jaded and inattentive.

Inattentive wouldn't help much, though, if we were locked in a cage. Plus, they'd have A.I.s monitoring us. A.I.s can get as bored as people, but they'd keep watching because they didn't have anything else to do.

"Welcome to your new home." Harding was gloating. Apparently he'd chosen this opportunity to abandon Mjolnir. His shiny new uniform had the crossed spaceships of the Security Corporation navy rather than the star and planet of the station-side branch.

I stared at him, trying to get my bearings. One moment I'd been sitting at a café, the next I was waking up in a slave pit.

I hadn't eaten anything with Harding so I suspected the cuffs he'd slipped on me came equipped with a contact drug or nanobes. Probably nanobes because my implants were down... again. Not that I was likely to be doing a lot of calling from somewhere in the middle of space, but I guessed it made sense to disable the girls' implants. It would make them more dependent on their future masters and reduce the chances that they could conspire without being noticed by the A.I.s.

Harding couldn't, though, have counted on the implant upgrade I'd bought myself. Now I needed to figure a way to use that to my advantage.

So I ignored Harding and stared around. If my sister wasn't here I was completely lost ... but then I spotted her running straight for me.

Shena threw her arms around me. "What are *you* doing here?" she whispered.

She had one black eye, a big bruise on her thigh, and her right hand was swollen to double its normal size. And she looked pissed. "You got away and then you let them catch you?"

63

I wasn't sure how she figured that out, but of course she was right.

"Mom and dad are gone. It's up to me to—"

"To what? Become a sex slave too just because they caught me?"

Put that way, the logic of my case wasn't especially strong.

"As long as we're together, we can figure something out."

"I've been *trying* to figure things out." She pointed at her face. "How do you think I got this?"

"I assumed it was from when Security raided the lab."

"That would be, oh, wrong. It happened here. I tried to take apart one of the bots delivering our meals. Some sailors objected."

Anger washed over me, so hot I wondered I didn't catch fire. Yeah, Shena could get on my nerves. Yeah, there had been plenty of times when I wished I was on the other side of the galaxy. But she was an eleven-year-old girl. Nobody had to hit her. Nobody had to abuse her. They'd done it because they wanted to. And because I hadn't protected her like I'd promised our mother that I would. "Shena, I'm so sorry. I…"

"It's not your fault they're creeps. It's your fault they caught you when at least you could have gotten away."

"Okay, I get it." I got that I'd put my life in danger for a girl who wasn't even close to being grateful. Then again, how grateful should she be considering what a mess I'd made out of things? I consoled myself with the possibility that maybe she'd be at least a little more grateful if I actually managed to get her out of this mess.

Harding leered at us. "Great news, girls. You're not the only ones getting off that miserable platform. I'm coming with you."

From the amount of gold braid on his uniform, it looked like he'd gotten the promotion he'd been whining about—thanks to me walking into his trap. I wouldn't have guessed teenage girls were that rare but he seemed happy.

He gave us the grin he'd used when we were in the lab … the grin I'd always assumed meant he was stupid. I finally realized he just used it to hide his true disgustingness.

"What?" he continued. "You're not going to thank me for putting you together with your sister? It is what you asked for, isn't it?"

"Hey, Harding," Shena said. "You can stick your—"

I put my hand in front of her mouth. Not that she wasn't saying what I felt. I just couldn't see how name-calling would help.

"Wise." He nodded to me. "I could make your trip a lot more pleasant … or less."

We were probably safe from Harding or the other sailors doing anything really permanent to us while we were on the slave ship. A girl with a broken arm or who'd been sexually mistreated wouldn't have as much value to the perverts in the market for untouched teens. Unfortunately, the sailors could do a whole lot of things that wouldn't leave permanent physical damage but would be disgusting or worse. If Harding wanted to torture us a little, nobody would stop him.

"You know we trusted you." I figured to play along. I couldn't figure any percentage in making him mad.

"Yeah." Another goofy grin. "I feel real bad about that."

I didn't think he felt bad at all. I thought he was a sociopath who didn't care about anyone but himself.

"If you feel so bad," Shena gestured at the floor, "maybe you could at least get us real beds." A couple of blanket rolls scattered on the steel cage floor suggested that we were supposed to sleep where we were. Which was more bad news. I'd assumed we be taken somewhere with either private chambers or even real cells like an old-time prison. With nothing but a common area, we would be under observation all the time.

Harding put on a sad face. "Sorry. Regulations."

"Is there anything you *can* do for us?" Shena had apparently picked up on my idea of playing along. "Anything at all?"

Harding chuckled. "You take care of me, I'll take care of you."

"We'll be good," Shena lied.

He reached through the bars and patted her on the head then groped for her butt. "I know you will."

My stomach was empty, which might have been the only thing preventing its contents from erupting. I was so tempted to take Harding's arm and break it in ten pieces that my body shook.

Hurting him, though, wouldn't get us out of this mess. And Shena was sacrificing herself, deliberately distracting Harding, and anyone else who might be monitoring us, for my benefit. I owed it to her to use that distraction

I restarted my implant, put its nanobe healers into high gear, then strolled around the slave holding cell.

I didn't see any cameras but that didn't mean anything. There could have been a thousand microscopic cameras scattered everywhere, and I figured there were—some of them original equipment, the rest planted by individual sailors who wanted to get a private look at the girls or create videos they could sell to perverts too poor to actually buy a girl.

The girls would need a lot of cleaning up before they could bring much of a price. A couple had actual whip marks on their backs proving that somebody wasn't too concerned about damage. One, a tall blond, writhed on the ground, repeatedly slamming her head against the dura-ceramic floor. A puddle of blood in front of her indicated she was doing real damage—and made my mouth water.

It took a real effort to force my gaze away from that puddle of blood—after all, if nobody else wanted it ...

Near the cell door, a girl with dark hair and skin, dressed in what looked like a plastic diaper and a thin strip of fabric around her non-existent breasts over a transparent skinsuit, was signing away ... to nobody I could see.

I watched her fingers for a moment. Each word was clear but the way she strung them together didn't make any sense at all. It probably gave any human monitor fits but I figured a Security A.I. would be fascinated, its programming convinced that there was a pattern. Maybe, just maybe, that would be useful. If the A.I. put the bulk of its computational power into deciphering the indecipherable, it might have a little less attention to spare for the rest of us.

I was grasping at straws, of course. Then again, straws were all I had. We were in a slave pit on a ship that had obviously been carrying slaves for a very long time.

I glanced back to make sure Harding hadn't gotten up to more than patting Shena on the butt, then continued looking around.

As far away from the door as possible, a girl even younger than Shena was going through a dance routine ... at least that's what I thought at first. She was practically non-descript—no figure, lank brown hair that flopped in her eyes, and a standard skinsuit that was cranked a size or two smaller than she needed.

I wandered in her direction and noticed that, although she was disguising the moves well, she was doing tai chi. And tai chi was just a slowed-down version of Kung Fu. Maybe…

I nodded to her, but she ignored me.

Okay. I was looking for allies and so far I was coming up empty. My sister was mad at me, the head-banger probably wouldn't share blood, and the girl who might know something about martial arts, not that tai chi is exactly a martial art, wouldn't even give me the time of day.

Then I noticed tai-chi girl's eyes were milky-white. She wasn't ignoring me; she couldn't see me.

Which didn't make sense. Nobody *had* to be blind any more. Even the most basic implants would correct any eye problems less serious than the eyeballs actually being cut out. Either she had blinded herself and refused to let her eyes heal or, more likely, they'd blinded her and disabled her implants to keep her under control.

"Can you hear me," I whispered.

She kept moving, drifting from one posture to the next with the kind of musical fluidity I'd never been able to find in my kung fu no matter how much I'd practiced even though I knew what it was and occasionally saw it in my father's forms.

Yeah, it was pretty, but her movement was so slow it would be useless in an actual fight. It also helps to be able to see who you're fighting.

I shook my head. My brain was getting ahead of itself. We were locked behind steel bars. The only real fighting we were likely to face in the near future was against each other—and I suspected that if we did get into a fight, the slavers would gas us before we could damage each other too much. Once we were sold, our chances of fighting back would go down even more. Admittedly tri-ds aren't known for being completely factual, but I suspected they depicted the slavery thing pretty accurately. And the first thing a new owner would do was replace a girl's implants with systems slaved to the house A.I.s. The new implants could be set to override conscious decisions, cause pain, or force a recalcitrant girl into unconsciousness. They could also be distance-triggered. Step beyond range of the A.I. broadcast net and you die. Cuts down on run-aways. According to the tri-ds, one trick was to let a slave run away in front of the others. When they keel over dead, it makes for great discouragement. Of course if the house A.I. just happens to glitch out, you've got a dead slave but I suspected the rich perverts would just buy more.

The way I figured it, if I didn't want to spend the rest of my youth as a sex slave and then get turned into dog food, I'd have to do something before we were sold. Getting ignored by the blind girl wasn't helping.

"I'm talking to you, tai chi girl."

She nodded slowly, almost as if it were part of the form and sketched out a 'yes,' sign that blended with the brush-back.

"You know how to fight?"

She shrugged, then signed 'impossible.'

"Hey, Kari." Harding gave the blink people do when they're in their heads-up display. "Don't bother with her—name is Nara but she don't respond to anything. When they get her somewhere with decent meds, they'll wipe her and put her in a public share somewhere. Same as will happen to you if you don't make me happy."

I noticed he'd pulled Shena's tunic up and his hands were running over her stomach and heading lower, so I abandoned the conversation with Nara and headed back to him, gently tugging Shena away and putting myself in her place.

"You will take care of us, Mr. Harding, won't you?" I wanted to vomit but thinking about sucking his blood got me through the moment. Still, I'd rather whine and act like a baby than face a mindwipe.

Once somebody got wiped, they never recovered. The only person I'd seen who was mindwiped acted more like a bot than a human, and not a smart bot, either.

I was impressed, though, that Nara had resisted whatever threats and punishments they'd doled out to the point, even after they'd blinded her, where she'd forced them to decide she couldn't be used. The kid was tough—for all the good that had done her.

Harding stretched through the bars to pat Shena on the head, pinched my non-existent chest hard enough to leave a bruise, then headed toward the elevator.

I watched closely as he called for a car, dialing up my vision to see if he entered a code.

No luck. Instead, he crouched a little for a retina scan. I hadn't figured how to get through the bars of the slave tank yet. Now I knew that, even if we did, we wouldn't be able to signal the elevator to get out of the pit. We couldn't just sit in the cage and wait, but picking the lock and taking the elevator while nobody was looking didn't seem like a plan either.

Speaking of picking the lock... "Were you watching when he opened the door?" I whispered to Shena. "Is there a key mechanism?"

She gestured to a pad about three meters outside the bars. No way could we reach it even if we could figure out the codes.

Time for plan B. "What time do the lights go out?" I kept whispering. They probably had microphones that could discriminate conversation even over the babble and head-banging, but I *had* to talk, had to learn about my situation, and signing would be even more obvious.

Shena shook her head. "They never change the lights. You just sleep when you're tired and hope you'll wake up. Although lately I've been hoping I *won't* wake up. Seriously, what do we have to look forward to? We'll be sex slaves to some pervert until he gets tired of us, then we'll be sold to some brothel until we're worn out. Then they'll either throw us out on the street or kill us because we aren't worth the air."

I'd seen the empty eyes in Gardenia staring through their drug haze at the world. I hadn't really considered that I'd been looking at the winners—the people who weren't slaves, were able to move around, watch tri-ds, even try to find work at the docks or in sailor bars.

"Don't think that way," I whispered. "We're going to get out and we're going to be all right."

Shena gave me a smile that promised she didn't believe a word of it.

I wasn't sure I did either. I'd had this mental picture of getting Shena and walking away, just like I'd walked away from the hospital. Obviously, I'd been way too optimistic.

Chapter Eight

In the tri-ds, ships always sound alarms, make a big deal about firing up their drives.

Maybe somewhere this ship had claxons and ship officers speaking softly as they did ship officer activities. Whatever it had, nobody bothered sending any warning to the slave pit.

The ship went from perfect stillness of orbit to a hard, throbbing groan in an instant.

The slave pit's steel bars screamed as the ship went from the gentle false gravity of spin to full artificial gravity—and I felt as if a thousand kilograms of lead landed on my back.

Everyone but Nara collapsed with the massive weight of our own bodies. Like everyone, I'd spent my assigned time in the centrifuge-stimulator, but that was just so my bones didn't rot. I'd never contemplated the possibility that I might actually need to move around in earth-like gravity. So, like everyone I knew, I'd done most of my gravity training while sleeping. No secret vampire strength popped up, either. Being a vampire didn't seem to be helping me much.

"How long you think this lasts?" Shena gasped for oxygen as she snaked across the slimy deck. "Gotta be six G."

I double-checked with my implant and was distressed to learn that this was earth-normal. "Only one gravity," I gasped. "I'm betting they leave it this way." There wasn't a lot of point in cranking it up and then lowering it later.

I tried to sit up—and failed. "They're probably taking us to a slave market on a planet, not an orbital or small moon. Need to toughen us up for their customers—we wouldn't be much use if we broke—too easily, anyway." I was pretty sure the goal was to break all of us eventually.

At the moment, though, I didn't feel like I was toughening up. I felt like I was dying.

My heads-up registered red across the spectrum. I truly didn't believe they'd intentionally destroy their merchandise, but I'd been through a viral attack, a long trek wearing a sub-standard rebreather, and been doped by Harding. They probably did their calculations assuming healthy girls, not someone who'd gone through the wars.

A mental image of the puddle of blood under the catatonic girl came to my mind. It had been a long time since that cup of blood with Watten.

The two times I'd tasted blood, I'd gotten a surge of strength and also a fix of antibodies that my heads-up had celebrated. Yes, the idea of sucking blood was disgusting. Still …

I reminded myself that the girl wasn't using her blood—she was dumping it on the ground by banging her head. Surely she wouldn't mind if I helped myself to what she didn't want.

Was I rationalizing? Of course. Would I be able to help anyone, including the head-banger, if I didn't regain my strength? I didn't think so.

I felt as if I had a slag pile on my back as I clawed my way across the floor.

By the time I got to her, head-banger wasn't doing any banging, but the change wasn't an improvement. She lay on the ground sobbing for breath. What had been a small puddle of blood was now a pool and more dropped from a cut about an inch above her right eye. I figured she'd been in mid-bang when the gravity came on and she'd hit herself a lot harder than she'd intended.

I'd thought she was catatonic but she gave me a glassy stare as I writhed closer, then brought her hand to cover her chest.

Yeah, right. Even if I'd been attracted to girls, somehow this didn't feel like time to look for a date.

I ignored her feeble gesture and stuck out my tongue to lick her blood off the deck.

"What … are … you … doing?"

Okay, she could communicate. She didn't look like she'd be a lot of help in a fight but she'd be worse if she kept banging her head.

I ignored her question and concentrated on swallowing every drop of blood that she'd left conveniently lying around.

I'd gagged on the blood I'd drunk with Watton, but at least it had been clean. Licking the deck, I was getting old filth, sweat and grease, rust, urine from probably a century or more of slaving, along with a bit of blood.

My nose quivered, my mouth involuntarily forced itself closed and my stomach rebelled at the taste and texture of the foul blend. I swallowed against my body's attempt to spew the blood mixture back up.

My heads-up indicators didn't budge as the blood hit my stomach.

I tried to lick up a bit more but couldn't seem to get my head moving in the right direction. Then black stars swam in front of my eyes obscuring the heads-up and the world went away.

****

"Crew will be coming soon."

I'd never heard the voice but I recognized it anyway. Nara whom I'd nicknamed *tai chi girl*, had the characteristic whine you hear in Earther tri-ds. Which explained why she'd kept at her tai chi even when the ship had gone to full artificial grav. Her voice also modulated weirdly—something else I'd heard in tri-ds—this was spy stuff, designed to baffle listening A.I.s.

"Who are you?" I tried to give my whisper a similar tone modulation.

"Just a girl."

Yeah, sure. Still, I didn't think she was an Earther spy. For one thing, Earth didn't have many resources any losing the war. The space corporations had beaten Earth-fleet back to the home stars a couple of decades earlier and since then, Earth worried about feeding its billions rather than messing with the slave trade. For another, Nara was barely in her teens, if that. Who would send a child to be a spy?

For a second, I fantasized about an anti-slavery underground, but I'd never heard of one. Then again, the tri-ds came from the same corporations who ran the slavery trade. Fantasy would have to wait. My queasy head finally calculated she'd said something important.

"What do you mean 'the crew will be coming'?"

She shook her head. "We don't have time for this. You asked me if I can fight. The answer is yes. What about you ... vampire?"

Before I'd lost consciousness, I'd been near death. I halfway expected my implants to have shut down from stress. Now, to my surprise, I didn't see any red in my heads-up from my implant—although there was a lot of amber, especially in the bone density and muscle tone sectors.

I ignored the 'vampire' part of her question. "I'll be weak in this gravity."

"This gravity is what we've got. The crew will be used to it."

I'd spent enough time in the lab centrifuge to know how slowly my body responded to g-forces, so I was surprised when one of the amber indicators blinked to green. Apparently the blood I'd taken, rotten and filthy though it was, was doing its job.

"You need more blood." Nara gestured to a girl lying unconscious on the floor. "Take some of hers."

I wondered how a blind girl knew where the rest of us were. Had she felt her way around the whole cage? Could she keep track of us by hearing? Still, there was a girl where she'd pointed so she had to know something.

"You're kidding. What am I supposed to do? Bite her?"

Nara shrugged. "Isn't that the traditional way?"

"I don't know. I'm new to this. But I can't just go around biting people. It's sick and it's invasive."

"That's Cassie," Nara said. "She comes from Plauton. You know what that means, don't you?"

Plauton was a planetary settlement in the Asgard system. Gardenia traded with them some but not as much as you might expect from two colonies in the same system. Unlike Gardenia, which had always been about making money, Plauton had been settled by religious zealots who thought they could create paradise. I didn't know how well they were doing at paradise and I'd never actually met anyone from our nearest neighbor, but they supposedly believed that whatever happened during life was a sign of what their god intended for them in the afterlife. If that was right, being sold into sex slavery would not only mean a miserable existence while alive, it would mean something equally painful and degrading for the eternity afterwards.

"Their culture doesn't allow suicide," Nara said. "But she wants to die rather than get sold into a brief lifetime of misery. You'd be doing her a favor if you killed her now, before the sailors come."

"But ..." I'd thought about this, been fairly confident we wouldn't be mistreated. "...surely they won't want to ... uh ... damage the merchandise."

Nara shrugged. "Maybe not, although some of us are already ... damaged." She used her fingers to make quote marks around the word "damaged." "But if you were from Plauton, it wouldn't take damage-style abuse to damn you to hell."

Okay, I got the logic. That didn't mean I could make myself bite someone—especially an unconscious girl who'd never done anything to me. Maybe if I could get Harding in range ...

This time the claxons did sound and the slave ship shook itself like an Earther dog.

"Entering XD-space," Nara said. "If they keep the same schedule they've been running, we've got five minutes before the first wave of fun-seeking sailors hits. Frankly," she continued, "I'm planning on fighting no matter what you do. I'm like Cassie. I'm tired of being dragged around, tired of putting up with being fondled and prodded by a bunch of sailors who would just as soon use sexbots but are too cheap, and I'm tired of living in the darkness. I heard what your boyfriend said about me—and a mindwipe doesn't sound that appealing. I'd rather be dead than enslaved. Maybe you don't feel that way."

I'd complained to my parents that working in their lab without pay was like being a slave. But I'd been wrong. Neither my parents nor Captain Russart had ever programmed overrides into my implants that would kill me if I went somewhere they didn't want me. They'd never used my implants to keep me in a semi-vegetative and constantly compliant state. Faced with the reality, I thought Nara was right. Better death in a fight than the semi-survival of a slave.

Nara was also right about my effectiveness in a fight. My vision had cleared. I thought I could stay on my feet if the ship remained very still. But I was a mess. And five minutes wasn't enough time for my body to heal itself, even with my implants working full power.

"Okay," I grumbled. "I get it."

I hadn't expected Harding to stick me on a slave ship. That didn't mean I'd thought he would welcome me as a long-lost cousin and help me free Shena. Ronin and I had spent a full day brainstorming and using the auto-doc before we'd tracked Harding at Security HQ. In addition to my upgraded implants, I'd implanted a tiny calcium blade beneath the surface skin of my butt. Even a CAT-scan, assuming they went to the trouble of running one, would show it up as a bone spur rather than a weapon. At least that's what Ronin and I had thought.

Freeing the blade wasn't the most painful thing I'd ever done—but it came close.

Nara nodded, her blind eyes seeming to take everything in. Then she went back to her tai chi.

Even in an unlicensed lab in a bankrupt orbital platform in a backwater star system, everyone learns basic surgery. Low gravity doesn't mean tons of rocks can't fall and break bones. And outside of Gardenia, there weren't ambulances to call ... assuming you had insurance to pay for those ambulances at all, which most of us didn't.

In the tri-ds, vampires always go for the neck. I supposed that made sense if you want maximum blood and don't care about damage. With my limited training, a makeshift scalpel made out of printed bone, and an unconscious patient who just might start jerking once I sliced into her skin, I thought an arm would be safer ... for both of us.

Cassie's arm was scrawny and as dirty as everything else in the slave ship. Clearly my new friend hadn't used the bathroom facilities, such as they were. Whether this was because she didn't want to expose herself to the cameras or because she'd driven herself to unconsciousness as soon as she'd been captured, I couldn't say. What I could say was that she stank and would start growing mushrooms if somebody didn't clean her up.

"You don't have to do her." Shena managed to writhe over to us. "Take blood from me."

"You know what I am?"

"I saw what you did," she signed.

I considered but rejected the idea. Shena was small, young and weak. She wouldn't be much help in a fight, but she wouldn't be completely useless, either. My dad had made her go through the same kung fu lessons I had, although she was younger and hadn't had as many. Cassie, on the other hand, wasn't even here. She'd chosen to retreat not just from the prospect of slavery but from her fellow captives.

I didn't have a problem with her doing that, but it meant that when the sailors came, she wouldn't be fighting. She could help most by giving me the blood I needed.

"Squeeze her arm here." I pointed the spot to Shena who, for once, actually did what I told her. "And huddle over her like we're trying to see if she's okay." I hadn't forgotten the cameras.

My implant-enhanced infrared perception let me see beneath Cassie's skin.

An artery pumped fresh blood out and my hand trembled as a rush of hunger swept over me.

I suppressed that thought, though and instead located a blue vein.

I pushed against it with a finger … and watched it spring back. So far, so good.

Cassie didn't even jerk as I snapped off the protective edges that had kept the blade from slicing my rear end into pieces. Then I pressed the weapon's mono-molecule-sharp tip into the center of the vein.

According to what I'd learned in my first aid classes, veins seep rather pump blood in spurts. This vein sent a substantial stream of purple-red blood straight up.

I mentally cursed but didn't waste time, or blood, in letting words out. Instead, I clamped my lips over her arm and sucked.

Fresh from the source, the taste was still disgusting. I hadn't expected that.

Clearly, though, there was a difference between fresh blood and the stale blood I'd had before. My heads-up reacted almost instantly, the amber indicators fading to pale green.

I felt powerful, was practically overcome by a ridiculous urge to surge to my feet and bellow out my defiance of the sailors, their officers, and the Security goons who thought of young girls as economic commodities rather than as people.

Which would accomplish what? Certainly it would send the A.I.s into full alert. So, I suppressed those ridiculous urges. If Nara was right and the sailors were only seconds away, I'd have my chance to defy them without the need to grandstand. For now, we needed them to believe that they faced nothing but a bunch of children incapacitated by gravity way stronger than they were used to. They had to be overconfident because, no matter how strong I felt, we were a handful of girls, mostly unable even to struggle to their feet, and mostly incapable of fighting. As I saw it, there was me, Shena, who probably couldn't hit hard enough to do much good, and Nara... who said she could fight but was blind.

I sucked down another deep mouthful of Cassie's blood, feeling the energy flood my system like water reconstituting a dehydrated food-stick.

It still tasted horrid, but a part of me wanted to keep sucking, keep swallowing, making myself ever-stronger and more powerful. Cassie had given up, after all. I'd be setting her free of the pain and indignity of... I stopped myself short. Where had that kind of thinking come from?

Everyone knew that vampires were sick, constantly needing blood to replenish our antibodies, unable to control our most basic urges. Until that moment, though, I'd felt like myself. Like someone who needed a drug but was still me. Now, I wasn't so sure.

I thought my hearing might be sharper since I'd become a vampire but I still didn't hear the elevator approaching. I jumped when it gave the distinctive "bing," the doors slid open and at least a dozen crewmen—if there were women on the crew, they weren't part of this invasion—spilled out.

Chapter Nine

"**R**emember." Harding held up a hand to slow the on-rush. "These girls are innocent. You can touch and rub, but if you break them, and you know what I mean, your pay will be docked for years … and you might just join them on the auction block. Don't think just because you're ugly guys, nobody will buy you. They just won't use you for anything you'd enjoy."

He walked up to the steel bars and stared at me.

Come on. I tried to project. Hypnotism was supposed to be an innate vampire skill, and I really wanted Harding to walk into the cell, to try to touch my body.

Instead he shook his head. "Disgusting. I really expected more from you, Kari."

I couldn't see my face but I imagined it was as grimy as the rest of me, especially considering I'd spent an hour or so lying, unconscious, on what had to be the filthiest deck in space. Plus, I hadn't been completely neat while sucking down Carrie's blood.

Bad as I looked, the other girls had to look worse. They'd been locked here for longer and they'd picked up the stink of the place.

So, we were disgusting. That might not make us good enough for Harding but it didn't seem to bother the other sailors at all.

As Harding coded the elevator, one of the sailors pressed his palm to the Security panel on the wall and the steel door to the slave cage swung open.

"Wait until the elevator leaves, idiot," Harding fired over his shoulder.

It was good advice and it would have mattered if we'd been an armed and healthy squad ready to take advantage of our enemy's mistakes. As it was, nobody moved while the cell door swung open—and the elevator door glided shut taking our best chance with it.

With the barrier down, the sailors stared at us and we stared at them for maybe three seconds. Then the dam broke and they shoved their way forward while shouting crude suggestions at their victims.

"Stay back," I signed to Shena.

"I'm going to hold the door open." She'd only made it to her hands and knees, so collapsing across the steel gate's track didn't take much effort. One of the sailors kicked at her as he passed but for the most part, they seemed more interested in the girls who'd at least started developing figures... not that any of us had much to show.

I'd wondered what good Nara's slow motion fighting could do. In my dreams, she would accelerate, turn tai chi into kung fu, and slice-and-dice the whole herd of sailors.

So much for dreaming. I got something else entirely.

Nara seemed almost to ignore the men who came at her, continuing a solemn dance that seemed as isolated as the head-bashing moves of my first involuntary donor.

"Hey, check out blindie," one of the sailors shouted. "She's already doing them tantra moves."

I'd been certain she would speed it up. Wrong again. If anything, her tai chi got even slower.

Somehow, though, her dance worked, and not in a way that the sailor would have chosen. Men reached for her and found that she wasn't where they grabbed. She didn't seem to block, but they threw their punches and seemed to fall after them as she brushed a hand against the arm pushing the fist, directing the force to where she no longer stood—which often seemed to be where another of the sailors had ended up.

I could have watched her dance for hours. Except I had my own problems.

I'd been proud of my kung fu. None of the kids I'd met could touch me. My father was better than me, of course, but I'd sparred against adults and generally done well... scored by points, at least, although I wasn't big enough to really hit hard.

There was, it turned out, a huge difference between friendly sparring and angry fighting. And this fight turned angry about twenty seconds after the sailors had crowded in.

When they realized Nara's dance was not only keeping them from touching her but banging them up, they stopped trying to fondle us, stopped caring about damaging the merchandise, and started hitting.

And it wasn't Nara who got hit.

Angry sailors struck out around them, kicking girls who couldn't move from the ground, grabbing and punching those girls who managed to stand.

I blocked some punches, and brushed my little calcium knife blade against one guy's arm, creating a healthy, but really distracting, flow of blood.

Then a guy I didn't even see smashed my hand with his fist and my blade skittered across the floor.

So much for my attempt at matching Nara's dance.

I kept fighting but the sailors brushed off my counters and ignored kicks and hand-strikes that would have scored sure points in a match.

I saw the problem. I'd studied kung fu all my life and I'd learned a lot, but I'd also trained myself to pull back on my techniques. In a sparring match, nobody wants to do real damage. A little pain is part of the game but broken bones, ruptured groins, dislocated joints, and gouged eyeballs were all forbidden. Unfortunately, none of the sailors had taken that lesson.

"You hit like a girl," Shena yelled from her spot on the deck by the door. She wasn't fighting but I noticed she was blocking and avoiding strikes when she could. Fortunately for her, all the sailors were now inside the slave pit. Which wasn't so fortunate for me. I was surrounded and their punches were getting through my blocks and doing damage. The heads-up had gone all green after I'd sucked down all that blood but it was now flickering amber in several areas.

Instead of shouting back that I *was* a girl, I oofed when some jerk hit me in the kidneys. Damn, that hurt

Another sailor saw my involuntary stumble as his chance. He yanked a sap from a pocket and swung.

I didn't have to *think* about this—my father had spent years giving me nightmares by jumping from around corners or shadowy areas of a room and swinging one of a large assortment of weapons at me. Which had been annoying at the time but had made my reactions automatic. I jumped back, throwing an elbow as I did to take out the guy behind me. The adrenaline rush must have given me extra strength because I felt his ribs crack under the force of my strike.

My jump back was almost enough to put me out of the sap's range. Turns out, *almost* getting away isn't at all the same thing as actually getting away.

The sap slammed into my chest.

Pain shot through my body and my heads-up blinked red before cutting back to amber.

I shook off the pain, stepping forward and shooting a stiff hand, fingernails first, into the sailor's eyes while I trapped his short club with the other hand.

Jerking back from an eye-strike is automatic. Everyone knows how much a handful of fingernails in the eyeball would hurt.

But his predictable response let me bring my elbow down just above his elbow joint.

His arm let out a solid snap, his mouth gave a high-pitched scream and all of a sudden I was the one with the sap.

I'd learned the lesson from losing my little knife-blade so I wasn't going to let this weapon get away. A weapon, even if it wasn't much of a weapon, changed everything.

Strikes that had been too weak when thrown with an empty hand became devastating when I propelled the sap into exposed elbows, knees, noses, skulls and groins.

Of the twelve men who decided a bunch of helpless girls would be fun prey, three made it to the elevator and two of those were bleeding. The rest were unconscious … or worse.

"Took you a while," Nara said as she kicked a fallen sailor to unconsciousness.

"Yeah. Sorry."

Then the black spots filled my vision again. This was getting old.

****

When I came to, Nara had my lips pressed to the chest of a sailor pumping blood from a stab-wound in his chest.

I fastened my lips to that wound and drank deep.

I wouldn't dare admit it, but this blood was tasting good. This time I was able to drink it down without any problems at all.

I kept sucking until the sailor gave a sigh and sort of caved in on himself.

"You ... you killed him."

I spun around to see Cassie. Apparently she'd revived herself from unconsciousness, although I was positive she hadn't done anything to help in the fight. Now she was looking at me as if I was the bad guy in this story rather than the hero who'd helped keep her from getting groped, fondled and abused by a bunch of perverted sailors.

Well, maybe I was the anti-hero. Jumping some stabbed guy and sucking his blood rather than trying to save him could be defined as evil behavior.

I gave Cassie a bloody stare and walked over to Shena.

My sister grinned at me and shoved the steel bars open—despite everything, she'd managed to hold her position, blocking the doors to the slave pit from closing.

We didn't have free run of the ship—we'd need to deal with the elevator. Still, we could get out of the pit. If we'd fought that battle and still been locked inside, the situation would have been hopeless rather than merely desperate.

"Good job, Shena."

"Plus—" she held out my blade which I'd thought lost in the fight.

Some of the blood on it seemed fresh, which wasn't a surprise—and gave me a couple of ideas. I decided the obvious one could wait. If we could get control the elevator before whoever was in charge figured out what to do, we could keep them from using it to drop in on us. Using it ourselves to overrun the ship was a shot too long even for me to consider seriously. If we could get control of the elevator, though, they'd have to post guards against the chance that we'd use it. The more we could give them to worry about, the longer I figured we would stay alive.

I looked around at the unconscious sailors and chose one whose uniform had a couple of stripes, and kicked him in the head.

He moaned and glared at me.

"We gotta lock down the elevator."

He looked at me groggily. "Huh?"

I hit him in the knee with the sap—hard. I was learning not to pull my punches.

His scream made me feel a little guilty—but only a little. Nobody had held a gun to his head to make him go down and torture a bunch of supposedly defenseless girls.

"We gotta take the ship." Nara stared at me with her milky-white eyes. "Now. Before they get organized."

I could see the logic of her position. There was only one slight problem—it couldn't work. "Too many of them got away and by now they'll have notified the officers. So, if we ride up the elevator, they'll be waiting. No matter how good your kung fu is, you can't dodge bullets."

"I don't do kung fu."

"Yeah, whatever." I twisted my sailor's arm behind his back and forced him to hop to the elevator, then jammed his face in front of the retina recognition system.

"That you, Keith?"

"Tell them you're injured and you need assistance," I whispered. "Say anything else and I'm draining every drop of your blood."

He must have seen me with the other sailor because he shuddered.

"Got them locked in their cell," Keith said. "But I'm injured. Send down some help."

"That wasn't so hard," I whispered.

Before he'd died, my father had been working with me on choke-outs and pressure points. Seven seconds after I squeezed off Keith's carotid artery, he collapsed into unconsciousness.

A mag-lev elevator doesn't make much noise but it moves air, and the outgassing of displaced air warned me they were coming.

They thought they were being smart. They'd known Keith was under duress so they loaded up the elevator with half a dozen sailors with crowd control weapons in addition to the two medics with a stretcher.

Unfortunately for them, I hadn't expected them to fall for Keith's act, either. I knew about the cameras.

Nara and I hit them before they knew what was happening. Ten seconds after the elevator door opened, we had three stun guns, a bean-bag cannon, a couple of projectile side-arms, and eight more hostages.

"That has to be most of the ranged weapons on the ship," Nara offered. "We arm ourselves and head out, they won't be able to stop us."

It was a happy thought. I gave good odds it was a *wrong* thought. This wasn't some merchant ship with a few old projectile weapons left on board in case of a rickety pirate attack. Harding had walked on and instantly started giving orders because he was Security. That could only mean that this was a Security ship. I didn't need the experience with Russart's lab to tell me that Security always brings more arms than they can possibly need.

I shoved the stretcher across the elevator door so it couldn't close—which would, I hoped, keep it from being remotely called away or, at least, give us a warning if they had an override.

"By now," I said, "they already have to know that something went wrong with their counterattack—and they've probably got their A.I.s working to figure exactly what we're up to. First thing they'll do is rig up something to hit anyone coming out of the elevator."

"Second thing they'll do is gas us." Shena still looked pale and she had a lump on her head. Unfortunately, she was also right. In an ordinary ship, it would take hours, maybe days, to override all of the safety precautions and rig up something to knock a group of girls unconscious. In a slave ship, they probably drilled for exactly this situation.

Once again, I'd somehow miraculously survived the impossible only to find that my situation hadn't improved at all.

A quick look around showed that the emergency rebreather lockers were empty so we couldn't suit up.

"Maybe," Shena said when she saw my expression, "they won't think of gassing us. I mean, they wouldn't want to risk damaging their cargo."

By this time, they probably wanted to do some damage—if only to persuade the survivors to behave. Once they figured out they had a vampire on board, they'd be sure to kill me first.

"Gotta keep moving." I was quoting one of my dad's clichés from kung fu training but it seemed to fit.

"Yeah," Nara said. "Where?"

Chapter Ten

The ship's ventilation system featured tubing even smaller than that in the lab. Not even Shena, the smallest among us could wiggle inside.

Which meant we couldn't use them to move around the ship. It didn't mean Security couldn't use them against us. They could send bots through, gas us or even evacuate the oxygen from the slave pit area.

We did our best to head off any of that by stuffing both intake and outflow vents with clothing we made our hostages strip off. I couldn't help feeling a degree of satisfaction in closing the slave pit door on the semi-naked sailors we'd captured, letting them wallow in the stench and crud of the pit ... wearing nothing but their skinsuits. Turnaround, as they say, was sweet.

In the process of making the sailors hand over their clothing, we picked up a couple of extra knives, an antique pellet-throwing pistol, a set of brass knuckles made of real brass, and a few food-sticks. The sailors, in turn, picked up more bruises and knotted heads. I wasn't sure the guy who'd packed the gun was going to make it—he'd actually drawn and pointed it before I nailed him, but he'd forgotten to take off the safety. I wasn't in the mood to give him a second chance.

Stuffing sailors' clothing into vents was satisfying. Realizing that we'd cut the flow of air was less so. The instant we sealed the last of the vents, a sense of claustrophobia, almost as if someone was standing on my chest, swept over me. I knew we had enough oxygen to last for hours and my heads-up informed me I was safe. But I'd spent my life in labs and stations. For as long as I could remember, the hiss of scrubbed air had been an assurance of safety and any break in that a certain sign of disaster. Now, panic still made me want to claw out the wadding and breathe fresh incoming oxygen.

I used my enhanced implants to dampen my adrenaline overload in an attempt to chemically eliminate the panic. Then I got to work.

It wouldn't be long before Harding and whoever else was in charge figured out what we'd done and reacted.

So, I got on the phone.

"You owe me," Ronin announced.

I breathed a sigh of relief. He'd promised he would follow, but we'd struck that agreement when I'd still believed it most likely that Shena was somewhere in Gardenia. Ever since I'd resumed consciousness I'd been dying to call him—but had resisted the temptation because the ship's A.I.s would detect the communication and realize my implant was functional and that I had an ally outside the slave pit. "I gave you most of the fifty-thousand," I reminded him. "And paid off everything you owed Watton."

"Following you on some ship still wasn't part of the deal."

"But you did follow me onto whatever pit this is. And let me tell you, I'm grateful."

"This pit is called *Stellar Princess*. And yeah, I'm here. Which is why you owe me."

"Got it. I owe you. How'd you manage to get on board?" I had visions of him smuggling himself inside a shipping container of food-sticks but that wouldn't work outside of the tri-ds. A.I.s and sensors were too smart.

"Easy. I followed Harding when he brought you to the ship's shuttle. The *Princess* had a yeoman supervising the loading and he told me they were looking for crew. So, I signed on. I'm one of your oppressors now."

"Lucky for you, you didn't join the rest of the crew when they came down to have some 'fun' with the girls."

"My turn wasn't until tomorrow. You need a lot of seniority to make the first run."

That was discouraging. I looked at the eighteen men we now held captive. "So, how many are in the crew because we've got a bunch."

I'd hoped that would be most of them, but I had to keep reminding myself this was a Security ship, which figured to be both better armed and more fully manned than the average cargo ship.

The only other time I'd been on an interstellar ship was before Shena was born when my parents moved to Mjolnir. I had only a vague memory of green walls and loud noises from that trip.

In general, though, it wouldn't make sense to pay a bunch of guys to sit around and do nothing for weeks at a time, just so you wouldn't have to hire locals to handle the loading and unloading at landfall.

"Yeah, that's the funny thing. I mean, when they hired me, I figured there wouldn't be too many on board, right? I mean, why hire me if you've got crew spilling out of every bulkhead and doubling up on the bunks. What's a ship like this need sixty sailors for?"

Sixty? That left over forty to deal with. I looked around at the ex-slaves. It was still pretty much me, a blind girl and my kid sister. A couple of the others were moving around but I hadn't seen any evidence they could fight. "So?" I asked. "What have you discovered?"

"From what they're willing to admit, running slaves takes more manpower than other cargo."

I didn't see that. From the looks of the slave-pit, they didn't exactly clean things out often. They hadn't fed us since I'd been conscious but I assumed they'd just use food-sticks. Water and toilet facilities were built-in. "What for?"

"Well, if you're thinking it's not for your comfort, you're right. What I'm gathering, reading between the lines, is that there are some people out there who don't like slavery. So, if you want to run slaves, you steer clear of the planets and platforms they control. But there are other people who are more pro-active in not liking slavery. So, for one thing you need a ship with enough crew to man your laser-cannons and missile launchers to hold off anyone who decides he wants to shut down slaving operations."

"I'm picking up that there's something else, too."

"Yeah. It seems that the *Princess* does a bit of what they call 'freelance security.' You pay up or they raid your lab, hijack your cargo, steal your girls, or take your ship captive."

I rubbed my eyes—the black spots were threatening to come back. "Got it. They're pirates."

"They call themselves 'anti-pirate raiders'."

"Good for them. Any way you look at it, there are a lot more sailors and more weapons than I counted on."

"They've got everything from venom blowguns to matter-anti-matter annihilators to hit you with."

Well, I was making sense of why Harding had gotten on board with them. This was probably a step on some career ladder for ambitious Security types—and Harding definitely struck me as ambitious.

"So, Ronin." I lowered my voice and held my hand over my mouth so the A.I.s watching couldn't read my lips and the girls wouldn't panic. "We've got to get out of here before we suffocate."

"I don't know," he said. "Even if I could get you out of the slave-pit, what good would it do? You're outnumbered and outgunned."

"Work on it," I said. "And hurry. By the way, you do this and yeah, I owe you—big."

"Well, I ... hold on."

Harding's voice interrupted, booming from speakers in the walls I couldn't see. "Females in the slave-pit. Your resistance only increases your punishment. Surrender now and rely on Security's mercy."

Cassie looked around, then screamed in what she assumed was the direction of one of the microphones. "They've got a vampire. How am I supposed to—" Nara cut her off before she said more but the damage was done. Any surprise we might get from having a vampire in our midst had just been negated.

"A vampire? How did that ..." Harding sounded pissed. "Oh, hell. It's you, Kari, isn't it? I should have pressed the hospital for the whole story."

I opened my mouth to shout something rude but Nara put a finger to her lips.

"Anyway ..." If Harding was disappointed that I kept silent, his voice didn't show it. "...obviously our first concern is the safety of the crew and the innocent slave girls in the presence of a vampire. If you surrender now, Kari, I'll make sure that Shena is freed and safely placed with a family as a welcome child. No need for her to be exposed to the hardships of slavery."

Shena was shaking her head hard but I ignored her. "What about the other girls?"

"What about them? One of them just betrayed you. Most of the others did nothing during the fight. And the one other slave who fought is an Earth-firster."

I looked over at Nara who shrugged again. Earth-firsters believed that the whole purpose of space was to let Earth people live more comfortable lives. Over the past couple of centuries, Earth had equipped vast fleets to roam through space taking anything those left behind on Earth might want ... no matter what the space-born owners might think ... until the corporations beat them back into the Earth sector. Sometimes an Earth-firster got separated from his or her ship—which created great plot lines for the tri-ds. Apparently Nara was one of those.

In corporate-space, Earth-firsters might be a little more popular than a vampire ... but only a little.

"Give me a couple of hours to think about your offer," I said. "You're asking a lot."

"I'm only bargaining because I want to save lives," Harding said. "You can't get away. No matter how long I gave you, sooner or later, one of those plugs you put in the air circulation system will come loose or you'll faint from carbon dioxide poisoning or one of the other slaves will decide they don't want you preying on them anymore or one of the sailors will wake up and catch you by surprise."

"Well, none of those things are going to happen in the next couple of hours," I said. "So back off and let me think. I will—"

"Oh. Interesting." He paused for long enough that I thought the conversation was over. I was stripping one of the projectile-throwers when his voice came back. "So you managed to get your implants working despite my block and made contact with someone in the crew, did you, Kari? It seems that I've underestimated you on every turn. Well, no more. If you don't surrender in the next five minutes, I'll open the bay doors and we'll flush out the entire mess of you."

"I've got eighteen of your sailors here," I reminded him. "You explosively decompress this chamber, they die too."

"Which is why we're talking in the first place. Four-and-a-half minutes."

****

Four-and-a-half minutes was not much time. And I thought Harding was only giving me that because it would take that long to override the ship's safety procedures to vent an inhabited chamber into the void. I also suspected that if he finished defeating those safety protocols early, I could forget about the time limit.

"Ronin," I sent. "Can you cut through the bulkheads and let us out? Oh, and be careful. They know I'm talking to someone and they'll figure out it's likely the new kid."

"Yeah, I guessed that and went into hiding. I'll check my copy of the schematics."

Thirty seconds later, he sent the bad news. "Walls are too thick. With the equipment I can get access to, it would take me at least an hour to cut through. Assuming nobody noticed."

The laser-cutter we'd confiscated from the sailors would run out of power before it cut so much as a pinhole through the reinforced steel walls, which made me wish the ship were newer and had been built out of carbon fiber.

We were royally in trouble. Not only didn't we have the right equipment or any time, we also didn't have much agreement among our ranks.

"You have to surrender." Cassie apparently didn't think she'd caused enough trouble earlier and decided she needed more. She grabbed me and put all of her weight on me.

It was getting harder and harder to suppress the urge to suck blood—especially when people were touching me. Especially when those people were really annoying.

I circle-stepped away from her, which crossed her clutching hands against my chest and loosened her grip. Then I brought an elbow down on her right hand.

Anyone who'd trained with my father would have laughed off the strike. Cassie collapsed to the floor moaning and wailing. "We're going to die. It's all your fault. We would have been adopted somewhere and instead we're—"

I confess I just stared at her. I knew she was scared but I hadn't believed she'd really try to get us all killed.

Shena wasn't as flabbergasted as me, though. She'd never gotten into kung fu the way I had, but our father had made her train anyway. So, I wasn't completely surprised when she punched the annoying turncoat in the gut.

"Send me whatever schematics you can on the ship," I phoned to Ronin. "And hurry."

A few seconds later, a design of the ship popped up on my display.

I saw what Ronin meant. The ship had been built around sealable compartments. Each compartment had walls several inches thick. I thought that design was more common in military vehicles than freighters—which typically were designed with walls that could be collapsed or moved to match different cargo requirements. Which made me wonder if the *Princess* was more of a pirate than she was a slaver—not that I liked either idea.

If it was military, though … military designs tended to stress survivability. In a military ship, explosive decompression wasn't normal but it was something planned for.

I zoomed in on the slave pit.

"One minute left," Harding announced. "If you ladies want to survive, I suggest you mob the vampire. I'd hate for you to pay the consequences for her sin."

"Hyperventilate," I said. "Flush every bit of CO_2 from your system and get ready."

Cassie spit on the floor. "Oh, yeah. That'll work. Instead of dying in one minute, we'll die in three minutes."

I had to hand it to her. She stuck with her position even when it got her banged up. I would have admired her for it a lot more if her position was one that wasn't going to get us all killed.

"Everybody grab one of the cell bars and hang on." I checked the schematics one more time to be sure I had this right. Then I opened a channel to Ronin. "Get to compartment 7-G-as-in-Google and make sure the north-side door doesn't seal."

"You have a plan?"

I clutched the projectile thrower I'd grabbed. "Sort of."

"One that won't get us killed?"

"Not so sure about that part."

"Oh. Wonderful."

"Remember, you don't get what I owe you if we don't make it."

"I know you mean that as reassuring. It isn't."

"Okay, guys." I gestured to the bulkhead the schematic said was the outside wall. "When that side blows, follow me."

Nara looked confused and I took her hand and pointed it toward the wall I was talking about. She seemed so capable I forgot she was blind.

She nodded and grabbed one of the comatose girls.

Shena gave me a thumbs-up before going white-knuckle on the steel bars. Around me, the other girls clutched the weapons Nara and I had forced on them. They looked scared.

Well, they should be scared. I figured my plan had about one chance in a thousand of working—if we were lucky.

It seemed like the thirty seconds had passed several times and still nothing. "Keep hyperventilating." I matched my words with action.

"What about us?" The sailors were still in the slave pit—and since I hadn't been able to use the cutter to get through the walls, I'd used it to weld together the steel bars. Harding wasn't going to be able to open it remotely and get us mobbed from behind.

"That's between you and Harding," I said.

I gave one last scan of the schematic and saw that if Harding took off the exterior wall, he'd also open the pit to space. Which meant, I couldn't count on them staying locked up.

"My advice," I added, "is that you hang on for dear life. And if Harding really does open the wall, you stay put. You try to follow us, I promise that you'll die even before we do. And everybody buddy up with someone who's still uncon—"

I'd hoped that Harding would string us along, give us some more warnings, try to protect his precious cargo. I didn't have a clear sense of the numbers but if it was good business to haul twenty dirty girls across the galaxy, it should be good business to keep them alive.

Apparently he was more scared of the vampire than he was concerned about his profit margins. The bulkhead exploded off into space less than a minute later than promised.

The whole ship lurched and the graphene/diamond that made up the hull rang like a crystal glass... a sound that quickly faded as the atmosphere evacuated.

An entire wall of the slave-pit peeled away like the lid of an old-time sardine can and bright pinpricks of distant stars peered in on us.

I suppose it would have been beautiful if it hadn't been so scary.

All of the atmosphere tore out through the gaping hole, tugging on my clothes and propelling more than sucking everyone toward the void. The artificial gravity turned off as instantaneously as it had been turned on.

I tightened my grip and watched. There wasn't that much air in the pit, in space, everyone pressurized to about ten percent of earth normal, almost all oxygen—so the air's movement couldn't pull me out if I didn't let it. Not everyone was so lucky—or careful, though. One of the girls had her mouth open in a scream nobody could hear as she glided into the gaping hole that had once been our wall and floated into the void. At least four of the sailors joined her—either they'd still been unconscious, they thought their chances of rescue were better in freefall than in the pit, or they simply hadn't been willing to take the suggestion of a girl when I'd told them to hold on.

It was scary out there but we had no choice other than following the dying... ideally with a bit more control.

Chapter Eleven

Ronin and I had spent twenty straight hours in near-vacuum just a few days earlier—but there's a big difference between wandering the surface of a good-sized moon while wearing oxygen rebreathers and naked exposure to the void.

I exhaled with the explosion, figuring I'd rather run short on oxygen than blow out my lungs through overpressure. Even so, I felt my body pushing against my skinsuit as the pressure differential kicked in.

In something large like Gardenia or even our lab, an air leak would have only gradually depressurized the environment, which is why patches and makeshift solutions worked to keep the platform habitable.

Here, the air was gone in less than a second.

Once the wind from the outgassing died, I went hand over hand on the steel bars of our cell, following the visible cloud of frosting oxygen out the opening.

I gritted my teeth, grabbed Nara, who wasn't likely to be able to make the leap on her own, touch-signaled her to hang on, hand-signaled the other girls to follow, and shoved off.

My parents had old tri-ds of me doing the zero-gravity dance on the ship that had brought us to Mjolnir but I sure didn't remember it. If I'd picked up any skills back then, they were gone.

Moving in zero gravity didn't feel like swimming, it felt like falling.

If I'd been thinking straight, I would have pushed off gently. The gap between our open cell and the ship's next section was no more than three meters so I didn't need to move fast. But my lungs were screaming their desperate desire for air and the sailors who'd been expelled were thrashing their arms and legs as if hoping to swim through space. The time for thinking everything through was long past. Now, I just had to keep moving, keep to the plan, and pray.

The one thing I had going for me was that every ship ever built was covered with hand-holds.

Sure, most in-space repairs are done by bots, and any supervising sailor wears a tether-line. Still, nobody wanted to find themselves forgotten in orbit around a ship. I'd counted on finding handholds. I hadn't counted on hitting them so fast.

My sweaty palm slipped as I wrapped my hand around the grab bar to the nearby cargo pod, Nara's mass adding inertia to mine as the bar slid through my fingers.

The sweat froze on the hand-hold, tugging on my fingers and slowing me, but it wasn't enough.

I'd jumped at an angle to the ship so I couldn't reach the next hold, but I had a stocked weapon which was as good as a pole for my purposes. I stuck it out and snagged its tip under the second hand-grip.

As I pulled myself in, the other girls hit me, grabbing my clothes, pulling my hair, holding whatever they could to keep themselves from floating into space.

Although we were weightless, a dozen and a half girls meant a fair amount of mass—all of which I hauled down my weapon, then I dragged them all hand-over-hand along the grips to what I hoped would be a working airlock.

If Harding figured what we were doing and could override the external commands, if Ronin's schematic was wrong about this little detail, or if I missed another handhold, the whole pile of us would simply float into space. Maybe, I thought, we'd freeze together and have enough mass to gradually attract space dust, eventually becoming a star.

The thought was a little poetic. It wasn't especially comforting.

****

Years ago, when I'd first hacked the base maintenance A.I. in the lab, I'd figured out how to download the lab schematics and used them to manage my explorations. I'd followed clearly marked paths into dead ends, empty spaces where doors were supposed to be, barriers where nothing should stand, security traps the schematics didn't hint at. So, I had limited faith in Ronin's schematic.

The problem wasn't that engineers don't know what they're doing or that the construction bots don't follow instructions. The problem is, things don't stay the way they start out but nobody links the construction schematics with the maintenance bots that hack together patches, create new uses for old space, or react to unanticipated dangers. Trusting this schematic to be right was a gamble, but I was down to hoping for a long shot. My lungs hurt and a gaggle of girls hung off of me as if their lives depended on it … which they did. I figured a long shot was better than no shot at all. I sure didn't buy Harding's lie about finding a nice family to adopt Shena. Did he really think I wouldn't notice he'd used that same lie when I'd confronted him on the Hill?

The bottom line was, I wasn't real surprised when the exterior handholds were replaced by a smooth patch about two meters from the airlock.

I felt a little like an old-fashioned train engine as I tugged myself and my cargo of girls down toward the last handhold, signing them to grab on. Somehow, I had to get all of us across that gap.

Jumping was a really bad idea. No matter how hard I tried, I'd create at least some vertical momentum and would drift away from the ship.

Finally I touch-signed Nara. "I'm going to take your feet and push you toward the airlock. When you feel the ship's skin, feel around for the emergency release."

"Got it," she touch-signed back.

Not all the girls let go but Shena helped enough of them to climb off of my body that I could move. I strapped the projectile launcher to my body and then grasped Nara by the legs and swung her body over the gap.

Space is cold, but vacuum is almost a perfect insulator. Despite the near-absolute zero of space, my sweat wasn't freezing, and I had a lot of sweat. So, unfortunately, did Nara.

As I pushed her forward I lost my grip on her ankle.

Oh, hell. I resisted the urge to scream and stretched myself out, barely managing to snag one of her toes.

Nara was small but that was a lot of mass to put on one toe. I felt the tiny bones crack under my grip.

This would not be a good time for her to go into shock.

Then she grabbed the airlock hatch and punched the emergency button.

I could practically feel the relief behind me as the airlock door opened. The girls had to be running as low on air as I was but they wouldn't give up now that they saw our rescue so close. At least I hoped the airlock would be our rescue rather than just a pathway from one vacuum to another. If Harding was watching, he was probably pumping air out of the compartment right now.

I hooked my feet around the hand-hold and shifted my grip on Nara to her calves, hugging my body to the ice-cold ship. Between me and Nara, our bodies created a human bridge across the gap between handholds and airlock. If the girls weren't too far gone in panic, they could, I hoped, scramble over that bridge to the possible safety of the airlock.

My lungs screamed for air even though I'd hyperventilated enough that I *should* have been fine for at least a couple more minutes. Maybe the whole vampire thing with faster movement meant that I burned through oxygen more quickly than I used to. If so, I was in trouble.

I instructed my implant to tone down my adrenaline rush and urged the girls to climb across me and get into the airlock.

None of the girls looked good. Those whose skin was normally pale were were turning purple, and everyone's eyes bulged from the air pressure behind their sinuses. Only the one who'd floated off at the start, though, seemed dead. I hoped.

I glanced behind them to make sure none of the sailors were crowding us closely. Those who hadn't drifted into space were still hanging onto the slave pit bars, probably hoping that Harding would seal the hull breach and give them some air before they died.

That flank taken care of, I looked back at the airlock.

Come on, I sent the instruction mentally since my hands were too busy holding on to Nara's legs for me to even think about signaling.

Shena went across last, then I let go of the handhold and climbed up Nara's body.

The airlock was full of girls but I eyed a couple of spots.

"Leave me," Nara touch-signed.

I just shoved her in… after being sure I had a firm grip on the airlock door. I didn't want the equal and opposite reaction to send me into space.

Nara got the urgency and claimed one of the spaces.

I headed for the second when I felt clawing hands around my neck.

Cassie had somehow managed to hide herself on the other side of the airlock hatch. Apparently she had decided to take her chances with the vampire. And now she headed toward the one remaining spot—the spot I'd mentally put my name on.

The airlock was filled with girls and the hatch was slowly closing. My lungs whined and my heads-up, already amber, blinked red.

I eyed the spot I'd designated for myself. No way would it hold two of us.

Cassie exhaled, her breath steaming white against the blackness of space. Her eyes rolled and she thrashed at the hatch.

I thought about how she'd betrayed us, told Harding I was a vampire, urged the others to give up. If she survived, I was pretty sure she'd continue to be a source of trouble.

A quick look into the airlock showed that the girls were all looking inward, hoping that the inside door would open to a pressurized cabin rather than an evacuated cargo chamber.

I could shove Cassie off and nobody else would know.

Nobody but me.

She looked at me, her face filled with fear.

If I suffocated out here, what would happen to Shena? Sure, Nara was a good fighter, but she was blind and she wasn't Shena's sister. Shena was sensible—for a little sister anyway—but she was young and didn't have my experience with the world. The other girls would be more likely to listen to Cassie and surrender if I wasn't there to buck them up. And who else could communicate with Ronin? Nobody.

It would be best for everyone … maybe even Cassie … if I elbowed my way into the airlock and let the hatch close in her face.

****

I couldn't make myself do it.

Instead, I crammed Cassie into my spot and added my strength to the hatch closing.

A part of me wished she'd been the one who'd forgotten to hold on and floated into the void. But she hadn't and I still couldn't make myself murder her.

Instead, I was alone on the outside of a spaceship surrounded by the nothingness of space.

One of the sailors floated by, his face black, his eyes blown wide.

For a second, I couldn't control my panic. I'd end up like him, floating in space billions of kilometers from the nearest living human. I didn't want to die.

I hammered the airlock, banged my hand against the emergency door. I knew it was silly, knew I was burning oxygen faster than I could afford because of my senseless thrashing. None of that mattered.

The panic didn't fade but my martial arts training came back to me.

I'd lost count of the number of times I'd faced men I couldn't beat in my father's dojos. Men who had better skills and more strength than I had. I'd panicked dozens of times as they'd closed in on me while I froze up looking for some opening we both knew I'd never find. Way too often I'd stood there waiting as they methodically discovered the chance to choke me out or put me in a painful and often humiliating submission hold. Over time, I'd learned to control the panic, to use the adrenaline rush rather than let it use me.

I switched off my implants and relied on my inner strength to control my lungs gasping for air in the vacuum, bring my pulse down below normal to something approaching hibernation, flush the toxins from my system, use only the minimum force I needed to hold on to the access hatch and wait.

Airlocks are slow. They have to cycle air in, then vacuum it back out.

My fear told me it had been hours, that the girls had listened to Cassie and blocked the lock rather than risk taking the vampire in. Logic told me that it couldn't have been that long—I would be dead.

Black spots danced across my eyes and my fingers spasmed. If I fainted again, I'd be dead.

Just as I considered giving in, letting the vacuum take me, the airlock door finally cracked open again.

"Just go in," I told myself.

Easy to say but I'd apparently gone too far in shutting down my system to revive so easily. My body didn't respond to my desperate orders.

I was going to die out here with the stupid airlock open and waiting to save me.

A hand snaked its way out of the airlock just as I let unconsciousness wash over me. I knew no hand belonged there but my mind couldn't quite deal with the complexity. Instead, it shut down.

Oh, hell, I thought. I'm dead.

****

"Wake up, idiot."

I moaned. I had the worst headache I'd ever felt and my sister, always a tag-along, seemed intent on harassing me. Typical.

"Sleeping," I groaned.

"We've got to move," Shena insisted.

"You don't leave me alone, I'm telling Mom."

She didn't say anything for a moment. Could I have won that argument? Her silence seemed to say "yes," but a nagging feeling at the back of my brain said "no."

That's when I remembered my mother's body in the lab ... and the spaceship where I'd found Shena. I wasn't going to tell Mom anything, and if I didn't do what Shena told me, Harding would kill me and my sister just as he'd killed my parents.

I didn't want Harding to win and sure wasn't giving up. I forced my eyes open.

A dozen pair of eyes, one set milky-blind, peered down at me.

Nara ran her hands over my face, then down to my neck. "You don't look so good."

"Funny. I don't feel hot either."

"They'll figure out we're here and evacuate the oxygen again." Nara gestured at the compartment we'd entered. The schematic

Ronin had sent indicated it was a cargo area used for carrying environmentally sensitive A.I.s, which is why I'd hoped it would be pressurized. If Harding didn't mind evacuating the slave pit to kill me, though, he wouldn't mind risking a few A.I.s, either. So, yeah, we needed to get our rears in gear.

"Whatever your plan is," Nara continued, "we need to move to the next phase."

That was easy to say. Unfortunately, I was pretty much out of plan. Surviving the depressurization of the slave-pit had taken all of my energy up to that point. Since I hadn't thought we'd survive that, I hadn't wasted much time figuring what would happen next. Except, of course, for the very basics.

"We can surrender," Cassie said. "They only want the vampire. They'd let the rest of us—"

"What?" Shena demanded. "Let us be sold to some perverts on some planet where we can barely stand. I'm not sure that sounds so smart to me."

"Better than dying."

"You really think so?" Cassie was probably eight centimeters taller than Shena and had to outweigh her by a good five kilograms. But Shena got in the older girl's face anyway. "Because," she said, "that's not the way it looks to me. The way I see it, if we surrender, we get a few months of suffering and humiliation with some rich pervert, then we'd get mind-scrubbed and turned over to some low-budget pleasure palace where we'd be as good as dead except a whole bunch of not-quite-so-rich perverts get to use our mindless bodies. Now, remind me how that's so much better than fighting back? How is it better than if we just died now?"

"Help me up," I said, my voice a croak.

To my surprise, Cassie was the first one to offer a lift. Maybe Shena had gotten through to her in a way I couldn't. Pretty clearly my gesture of letting her take my spot in the airlock hadn't done anything to change her attitude. Of course, she probably hadn't even noticed.

I grabbed her hand, pretended not to see the moment of revulsion that crossed her face, and heaved myself up.

My eyes spotted again and a wave of dizziness threatened to sweep me away but I leaned against the wall and sucked in oxygen. "Okay," I gasped. "Let's go."

I made sure I still had the slug-throwing weapon I'd claimed as my own, checked that I hadn't bent its barrel while using it as a grappling hook, then called up Ronin's schematic.

"Anyone who wants to stay alive, follow me," I said.

The ship's fundamental design shouldn't have changed too much from when it had been built so I took a left, and accelerated into a stumbling jog. At least Harding hadn't turned the gravity back on.

"Someone coming from the north," Ronin reported.

"You at 7-G?"

"Yeah. Following orders, ma'am. And trying to stay ahead of the crew since you blew my cover."

"Sorry about that. Keep the door open."

"Easy for you to say."

Well, no—talking wasn't especially easy. Nothing was.

I realized my fingers had clamped themselves onto the projectile-thrower—to the extent that they seemed immobile. Which wouldn't help much in a fight. So I called up my implants … again … and forced my fingers to flex. I'd feel like an idiot if I dropped the weapon before I shot it. Yeah, I'd probably drop it if I did manage to fire it, but I'd prefer that happen *after* I took care of Harding.

I tried to run faster when I heard the sound of a scuffle ahead but lost my balance and skidded across the floor before rolling back to my feet—thank goodness for low gravity and thousands of controlled rolls from back when my father had tried to inculcate basic fighting skills in me. They, not any particular virtue in me, made my recovery automatic.

"Move out of the way, punk." As I turned a corner, I spotted a couple of big sailors shoving at Ronin.

"Captain Harding said to keep this hatch clear," Ronin insisted.

It was a pretty good line—after all, what sailor wants to bother the captain to confirm orders.

"Funny," the bigger of the sailors snarled. "'Cause he's telling me to get it shut—now. And he wants you to come with us,"

Okay, Ronin's line wasn't quite good enough after all.

By then, though, I was in compartment 7-G. Ronin didn't have to face them alone … and I had my gun.

I leveled my weapon. "Back away from the door."

Instead of backing, the sailor dropped his grip on Ronin's shoulder, turned and ran.

In tri-ds, gunshots are low-pitched roars. In the helium/oxygen mix of the spaceship, it's more of a squeak.

I looked down at my weapon as the sailor cartwheeled away. I hadn't fired.

"I hate it when people don't do what you say." Shena growled at me. She had a pistol-sized weapon rather than the big shoulder-aimed thing I had, but she'd managed to make it work, which was more than I could say.

She gave Ronin a doubtful glare. "You sure he's okay?"

"Yeah, he's our ace in the hole."

"Some ace." She pushed ahead of me.

"Let me take lead," I shouted. "I know the way."

"I hate it when you glory-hog," Shena said. "You think I can't follow the markers to the bridge?"

For someone who'd shot a sailor for disobeying me, Shena seemed remarkably reluctant to follow instructions. Then again, she was my sister.

I checked to make sure the other girls had caught up, then took off. "Grab a weapon from the dead guy," I signed to Ronin. "And move."

Two seconds later, I heard another gunshot. "All right, he's a dead guy now," Ronin sent. "Faking it before."

That really wasn't what I'd meant.

I reminded myself that this was a slave-ship. The crew knew they were shipping slaves when they'd signed on. They took turns abusing the girls they were shipping. Ronin hadn't shot an innocent victim.

I might have convinced myself if my mouth hadn't been watering over the scent of blood.

Ronin caught up with me as we approached the bridge and handed me a canister.

"What's this?"

"Remember when they tried to gas you?"

"Yeah."

"I was supposed to place one of those canisters."

I grinned and took it from him. "Slow down, Shena," I shouted. "Ronin has a surprise for our loving hosts."

Chapter Twelve

Unlike us, the bridge crew didn't expect to be gassed. Shena's hands were small enough to slip the canister into the ventilation system while Ronin rounded up rebreathers for all of us. That took maybe a minute since we were out of the slave area and the ship had its emergency equipment intact.

"Pull the release," I said.

For once, Shena actually obeyed my instructions and the gas hissed into the ventilation ducts.

Cassie rolled her eyes back and collapsed. Either she hadn't properly fastened her rebreather or it hadn't worked. The rest of us looked… well, like a bunch of girls who'd been on the wrong end of a fight.

"Let's go," I ordered.

Ronin's job on the ship was moving cargo and he'd found us a forklift. I hopped into the driver's seat and headed for the bridge door.

It took three hits before the door folded and I was pretty shook up from the collisions, but we finally got it open.

Screaming like a high-pitched, pint-sized banshee, Shena was the first one through. She'd fired her weapon five times before I joined her and saw that the fight was over.

Whatever forces Security had left hadn't hung around to duke it out. The hatches holding emergency rebreathers still hung open but pools of vomit on the deck suggested that they hadn't gotten to the rebreathers before being largely incapacitated by the gas. Which, I guessed, was why they hadn't stayed to fight.

Every single control screen was smashed.

"Stop shooting," I told Shena.

"We are dead," Ronin said.

****

I slumped in the captain's chair. Four hours after the fight, my implant was still sending warnings and my headache just wouldn't go away.

It didn't help that I was so discouraged. Once Ronin had handed me the gas bomb, I'd been confident we could capture the bridge intact, with the officers still in place and under our control. Yes, the gas had surprised them, which is probably why they hadn't killed all of us when we'd broken in. But Harding, along with all of his officers, had evacuated on a lifepod leaving us every bit as trapped as we'd been when we were in the cage.

"The ship has to be going somewhere," Cassie said in a fit of optimism that seemed naive even for someone from Plauton. For better or worse, she showed no lasting effect from the gas. "When we get there, we can tell whoever boards us what we're escaped. They'll send arrest warrants for the slavers and—"

"They'll thank us for bringing ourselves in," Nara interrupted, "and start the auction."

Cassie shook her head. "But they *can't* just hold us as slaves. That would be—"

"What? Illegal?" Nara grasped Cassie by her head and gently twisted it from left to right and back. "Look around this ship, Cassie. Notice anything? It's not some unlicensed pirate vessel, it's Security all the way."

"But Security is responsible for fighting pirates and—"

Nara tightened her hands into small fists. "Security is in the business of making money. They fight pirates because shipping companies pay them to do it. And since they're out there anyway, they make extra money trading high-value merchandise. Well, guess what? Young girls are worth money. I'm betting that your parents didn't pay their insurance or broke some Security code or did something that makes it perfectly within their rights to seize and sell you ... and fighting back like we did will just mean that they treat us more roughly."

Nara was right. In the tri-ds, slavery is managed by unlicensed operators, and I knew there was a lot of that. But unlicensed operators tended to stay on their home planets or stations. Travel between the stars takes money. Pirates and big corporations were the ones who had that kind of money—and apparently there wasn't as bright a line between the two as the tri-ds implied.

In the tri-ds, merchant-heroes are always fighting off unscrupulous low-lives who want to roll them in port (probably where Ronin had gotten his ideas), exploring new planets, carrying vital technology to lost colonies, and rolling in wealth. But even in the tri-ds, space merchants never let morals get in the way of making money. They'd loot another ship, deal in slaves, hold a planet or station hostage, or do anything else if it brought them a few extra bucks. It might be illegal… on Plauton. But Plauton's laws stopped at the edge of her atmosphere. In space, laws came from who had the biggest guns and that, except in the small area controlled by Earth-fleet, meant the corporations. I was pretty sure Harding was smart enough to be sending us somewhere where those with big guns were fine about selling little girls to make big men happy.

Which meant Nara was right. If we didn't change our course, we'd end up in the same slave market Harding had intended for us. He'd probably even get his bonus if we showed up. If we managed to override the ship's navigation, we'd drift in space until Harding's lifepod made contact. Then Security would track us down ... and take us to that or some other slave market.

I looked at the smashed controls again, then rubbed my aching head.

"You're sure they wouldn't help us?" Cassie asked.

"She's sure," Shena answered.

"But then everything we've done has been for nothing. We'll—"

"*Kari* can fix it." Shena was always confident in her big sister's ability ... no matter how often I disappointed her.

"I think Shena is right," Nara said. "Think about it. This is an old military vessel, right?"

"Yeah?" We'd discovered original earth-markings on the inside of the ruined screens. At one time, the *Stellar Princess* had been part of Earth-fleet, back in the days when they'd thought they could beat the corporations and use the resources from corporate space to feed their billions.

"Military ships," Nara continued, "are designed to take a lot of damage and to be repaired by whoever is still alive at the end of the fight."

"They aren't," I pointed out, "designed to be captured by a handful of girls and escaped slaves."

"You'll figure it out," Shena repeated.

I think I would have found her confidence a lot more reassuring if I hadn't lost my parents, turned into a vampire, been tricked by a slimy turncoat, and then bundled into a ship that was heading for a slave-market. All in all, it wasn't a record that would give the unbiased viewer a good feeling.

Still, I wasn't going to give up as long as the other girls had faith in me. The other girls and Ronin, that is. I wondered what he made of finding himself the only male in a ship full of girls. Cassie was more attractive than me. And Nara was probably smarter. And Shena was, well, cute. Which left me what. The ugly step—

"Stellar Princess to Kari," Shena said. "Anyone home?"

"I'll see what I can find out," I said pulling my attention back from foolish speculation.

****

Although the Princess's officers had abandoned ship when we'd pumped gas into the bridge, not all the sailors had joined the exodus. Keith, the sergeant we'd made call for the elevator, had somehow managed to hang on when Harding had depressurized the slave pit, and was the only captive who'd survived from the original group. There were other sailors, though, scattered throughout the ship. I suspected they'd be happy to sweep us out, bring the cargo in, and get a reward for the recovery of the ship and the girls.

Of course I'd been right about Ronin causing problems. For one thing, Shena seemed to have taken a serious crush to him. For another, Nara was convinced he was just another male ... ready to sell all of us into slavery if he had a chance. Considering that Ronin had wanted to murder sailors for money, I couldn't say that Nara was completely wrong in suspecting his basic morality.

The sailors knew the ship and had plenty of time to find weapons. So, I insisted that everyone stay together in groups of three ... all of them armed.

My team was me, Shena and Ronin.

Shena held onto the pistol slug-thrower she'd shot at (and missed) the sailor with. Ronin had a big laser-cutter—the one he *hadn't* missed with. I had traded my shoulder-mounted monster for a little plasma pistol that, I thought, was more likely to incapacitate and knock unconscious than kill—I was tired of killing.

We'd just come from the mess hall—at least we had enough food-sticks to feed us for years with constructors to make more—and were heading for the medical center.

"You don't look good." Apparently seeing all that medical paraphernalia inspired Shena to want to use it.

I stumbled over the five centimeter lip at the base of the airtight door then glared at her. "I'm fine."

"You're not fine. You need blood."

"Okay, so I need blood." I waved my arms. "Here we are at the medical station. You see any blood handy?"

Ronin poked at some of the equipment but didn't turn up any big flasks of blood—which didn't surprise any of us. Implants handle most minor medical emergencies, so a medical station is more about adjusting implants than it is about actually dumping new blood in anyone's body.

"Maybe," he said, "we could adjust your implants to let you make your own blood."

"Brilliant. You don't think, just maybe, if it were that easy to cure vampirism, they would have done it in the hospital, or that quack we went to that sold us the upgraded implants would have done it?"

"Well hello Ms Snarky."

Yeah, I deserved that.

"Take some from me." Before I could apologize, Shena yanked up her sleeve to display her scrawny and bruised arm.

I glared at her. "I can't do that."

She grabbed me by my two elbows and turned me so I faced her. "I know you think you're being noble—sacrificing yourself for the good of others and all that nonsense. Just like you did in the airlock when you almost died and would have left us stranded because only you had the schematics and only you could talk to Ronin about where we were going. Well, it was a dumb idea then, but at least you had a chance of survival there. Now, you don't have a choice. You either get some blood or we all die."

"Oh, come on." I waved my arm at the medical equipment. "Look at this. We can all replace our implants here. That'll make any of you as good as me. Better, really, because you're not vampires."

"You're deliberately missing the point."

"Well I—" I meant to go fire back something clever but all of a sudden I was sitting down … and there wasn't a chair in sight.

Ronin and Shena caught me before I hit the ground and navigated me to one of the examination tables.

"Cassie will talk them into giving up if anything happens to you," Shena said. "So, I'm not letting you die no matter how bad you want to destroy yourself."

I hated to admit it, but she was right. Nara could fight better than me, but if the other girls had seen her in action, they really hadn't gotten how good she was. Just because I'd known Harding would try something, because I'd been lucky enough to have my implants go bad and make the money to upgrade them, and because I'd been the one to locate the Hasro stash and make some money from the drug lords, the other girls depended on me.

"Here's the way it's going to be," Shena said. "We'll take rotations. Every day, one of us gives you a quarter of a liter of blood … for a start. If that's not enough, we'll give more."

I wasn't thinking quite straight but that sounded dangerous to me. "And we're all be anemic."

"Yeah, so?"

"Thing is," Ronin said, "we have a medical station. We can fix everyone's implants. With good implants and enough to eat, replacing the blood shouldn't be hard."

"You're donating your blood, too?"

He grinned. "Remember I said you owed me?"

I nodded.

"Well, I've got to protect my investment."

I wondered if I was imagining the quick look he gave my sister. Had he seen the obvious crush she had on him? And how did he feel about her? My feelings were all confused all of a sudden … the only explanation, obviously, was my lack of blood.

The medical station was bigger than I would have guessed from the size of the ship, but when I thought about it, that made sense. Earth spent everything they had building a fleet that could, they hoped, conquer the human sphere. They'd needed to keep their sailors alive. Once Security had turned to slaving, they would have needed to keep the medical up since they disabled the implants on their cargo. After all, the price they could get for the girls they delivered would depend on our health.

Ronin strapped Shena down on another examination table while I tried to stay conscious enough to keep my weapon pointed at the door just in case one of the loose sailors decided this was his time to be a hero.

There was a blank datastrip at the base of Shena's table and I had a flashback to the hospital … the sheet covering the jell-bed and the data strip. I grimly pushed away those memories. Shena wasn't going to become a vampire, she was just giving me a little bit of blood.

"A quarter liter, right?" Ronin said.

"Let's start smaller," I said. "Maybe 2.5 deciliters."

He nodded, then brushed his hand over the data strip. Like me, his implants were still operative so he could give instructions.

Which reminded me… "Have it fix her implants while you're at it."

He nodded again and brought his finger back to the strip.

The machinery whined and a small bot climbed out of the cot and clamped itself around Shena's arm.

She gave a little wince—military hospitals aren't famous for their sensitivity to pain—then managed a small smile. "I trained too. I can take it."

I hoped so.

I looked away and tried to think of something other than that little tube of purple blood.

Which shouldn't have been hard—I had a lot to think about. After all, we were hurling through space, making hyperspace jumps every couple of hours, heading toward whatever destination Harding had programmed into the ship's A.I.s before he'd smashed the interfaces. Unless I could figure a way out of that mess, drinking blood just meant I'd live until when Security re-captured the ship and sold my friends back into slavery.

It was just that my thinking didn't seem to lead anywhere.

Shena sighed as the bot retracted its probes from her arm, then jerked as if she'd been hit with an electric shock.

"Hey." She said it, but the message echoed in my head. "Got my phone back."

I nodded. "Thanks, Ronin."

"Shut up and drink the blood."

The surgery bot wasn't designed to let someone open it up and drink the blood, but it didn't resist Ronin's commands when he ordered it open for cleaning. He extruded a glass tube from a medical constructor and handed me both.

I put the tube in the bot's holding tank and sucked up the few precious drops of my sister's blood.

I was getting used to the taste. Knowing I was sucking down Shena's blood gagged me, but my headache receded with each sip.

The indicators in my heads-up flickered from red to amber to green. Despite myself, I smacked my lips. A heady sensation filled my body—I felt as if I could fight an army of Security goons and win.

"That enough?" Shena still looked worried.

"Yeah. Thanks, sis."

She shrugged. "Not like you haven't done a lot more than that for me. I can't believe you deliberately let Harding catch you. I never would have been that brave."

"That idiotic is more like it." Still, her praise made me feel good. Yeah, I was a vampire, but that didn't make me all evil.

"We should get the others in here," Ronin said. "Fix their implants like we did Shena's. We'll be a lot safer when we're commed together."

He fingered the data strip and I had a brain flash. "Give me one of those data strips, will you?"

****

Good design says that A.I.s are kept segregated. But good design also requires massive redundancy.

I ran my finger across the data strip, probing it with my implants. "Authorization required," it told me.

Well, that was discouraging ... but not surprising.

I'd been hacking my way around computer security since I'd been five. So, I was hopeful when I started nudging my way around.

"You have a plan, right?" Ronin said after a while. "What can we do to help?"

"Besides protecting me when I'm a million kilometers away and feeding me blood?"

"Yeah, besides that."

"You know anything about A.I. hacking?"

He looked at me helplessly.

"Okay, stick with shooting anyone who attacks."

"What's the problem," Shena asked.

"The A.I. needs some sort of authorization."

"Ronin didn't have any problems making it work."

"It's multi-layered. Anyone can do the lowest level, which is basic medical procedures like implant startup. If you want anything more complicated, you need validation."

She nodded. "Makes sense. If you hurt yourself during the night, you want to be able to get a quick repair. But it won't let you take more than a few doses of Hasro without permission."

"I think it knows more than just how to do first aid, but I can't get through to be sure."

"I guess," Ronin said. "You never know what's going to get shot up so you make sure every A.I. can do every job."

"But I can't get it to respond. I don't know enough about the doctors who ran this station to guess their passwords and, of course, I don't have their retina scans so I can't—"

"But do you really need that?"

"I told you, I can't get through."

Shena reached down into her examining table and yanked an A.I out of its socket.

"What do you think—"

She took the glass tube from the equipment stand where I'd left it and probed the device, finally slipping the glass between the A.I.'s base and the fiber optic leads to its power antenna ... and jerked.

The data strip went dead in my hands.

"What the heck? That A.I. doesn't just control your table, you shorted out the entire medical center."

"Hope I can get it back."

She poked at the fiber leads. "Hmm."

I reminded myself that she was only eleven. When she was fifteen, like me, she'd learn to think before she acted. Maybe. Assuming she survived to fifteen. Right now, surviving more than a few days sounded unlikely.

With most A.I.s, yanking out the optic connectors would destroy something. Military equipment seemed different. After about four minutes of trying, Shena made a triumphant noise and the A.I. lit up.

"Try it now." She practically screamed the words.

"Why should anything be different?" Just because I asked the question didn't mean I wasn't doing my best to interface through the data strip.

"I just hope it will be."

Yeah, that was reassuring.

It took longer than I'd anticipated for the A.I. to come up and I felt a bit of guilt. A.I.s aren't *alive* in any real sense, but they weren't just dumb computers, either. Over time, they learned, adapted, developed differences. In the end, they had personalities and Shena had just wiped one out.

"If it reboots," Ronin put in, "it may be in its basic configuration. Like, maybe, asking what we want it to be. Surely it'll sense that the ship's other systems are down and ..."

The data strip sent a garbled message, then went dead again. "Yeah, or maybe it won't reboot."

"That is a chance we're taking," Shena admitted.

A chance *she'd* taken. I decided not to point that out. She'd feel guilty enough if she'd destroyed the ship's medical station for nothing, especially before we got all the other girls upgraded to military implants.

"Good thing," she continued after waiting long enough that I knew she'd been sure I was going to jump down her throat, "I got my turn with the medi-bot before I, uh, repaired it. You can bite the others but it would be gross for you to bite your own sister."

Finally I had to admit the truth. Her 'repair' had destroyed the medical A.I.

Gross as it would, be to bite my sister, it would be even more disgusting to be stuck on a ship with a hungry vampire and a dozen victims. One by one, I'd drain them dry, leaving them for dead.

Once I was the last one alive, I'd gradually lose function and the microbes that eat up the dead would attack me alive, grinding me into dust.

It would have been better, I thought, if I'd just refused her blood, let the vampire virus do its work.

Chapter Thirteen

After a day of panic, Nara's team located a spare medical A.I. and we were able to boot it and set our own security. During that day, I didn't bite anyone but my headache came back.

I needed blood often. What worried me was that I seemed to need it more and more often.

Once we got the new A.I. figured out, we cycled all of the girls through, replacing their ruined implants and giving them fully functional adult military upgrades that let them be manually reset in case they were captured.

Ronin had tried to insist that Nara go first but she refused. It wasn't until all of the other girls had their implants restored that I realized the problem. Nara was an Earther. On Earth, implants were reserved for the rich and for the fleet. With its overpopulation, Earth didn't feel the need to keep ordinary people alive. I hadn't known, though, that it had become some sort of moral position.

"I do fine," she insisted. "And I don't want to become dependent on some devices that the slavers can take out."

"The slavers could cut off your arms," I reminded her. "So you think you should cut them off yourself just because they might do it? Refusing the implant is just as silly."

"I was afraid of my first implant too," Cassie said. "A lot of people on Plauton don't get them because the prophet didn't have one."

Ronin opened his mouth, undoubtedly to tell Cassie how stupid that sounded, so I gave him an elbow in his side. If anything, Cassie's approval would persuade Nara to do the right thing.

"With the implants, you'll be able to respond if your team gets into trouble," Shena said. She was incredibly proud of her new adult implants.

"Fine," Nara grumbled.

****

She might have said she was ready but actually getting her into the med-center took a lot more arguing. It seemed she always had something critically important to do, something that meant she couldn't come to the med-center right that moment. "This was an Earth-military ship," she reminded me. "Which means that there's got to stuff hidden away somewhere. Earthers don't trust anyone."

Finally I twisted her arm, telling her she could look for a way out of the mess we'd gotten ourselves into better if she could actually see.

For most of us, updating an implant was a simple matter of sucking down a sicky-sweet nano-infused drink or a quick I.V. hookup That's because we already had basic implants building from the time we were in the womb. The brain and the implant evolve together, the way it's supposed to be. Even if her accent hadn't given her away, the lack of even a rudimentary implant would have told anyone in the universe that Nara was from Earth or from some primitive world like Plauton.

Earthers who went into their navy, though, had to get implants so they could control the ship. And this ship's med-center had the equipment to force implants into brains.

Nara screamed when the probe went up her nose, searching for her brain, the med-table holding her head firmly encased while her body strained against the gel.

"I guess Earthers don't want their spacers to think implants are a good idea so they make sure it's painful," Ronin said.

Her screaming continued long after I was sure she was unconscious and I could only imagine the implant carving out hunks of brain and implanting itself onto her skull.

Ronin, Shena and I took turns sitting by her med-table as what had been a five minute procedure for the other girls turned into a multi-hour ordeal for Nara. When I was on duty, I stuck one of my hands in the gel, touching a finger to her hand. I wasn't sure if she was aware of the contact and was even less certain she would have wanted it, but it seemed the least I could do for persuading her to go through this.

Ronin was just reporting in for his shift when Nara twitched.

"She's not screaming," Ronin whispered.

I guessed that was good news.

Her eyes were shut but I saw movement under the lids. "Come on, Nara. Open them. Let yourself see," I murmured.

I wasn't sure if she heard me but she slowly opened her eyes. And screamed.

"Oops," Ronin said. "Spoke too soon."

I should have been ready for that. Nara had been without sight for a long time. Her brain would have adjusted to sightlessness, her neurons reprogramming themselves to use the information she did get. Now, her optic nerves were sending signals to neurons that just weren't ready to get them.

"Lights at ten percent," I ordered.

The med-center's illumination dimmed but Nara didn't stop screaming. That took another five minutes.

****

"I see everything twice."

Nara's voice was a husky relic but her words nagged at some memory in the back of my brain.

We'd been sitting with her while she screamed, finally turning out the lights altogether, but that hadn't helped. Her newly refreshed optic nerves had kept sending their messages even when they'd had nothing to send.

I'd almost decided this whole thing was a mistake and had started seeing if we could recode her implant back to blindness, which might have been possible but I hadn't figured out how. Then Nara gave that weird whisper.

"Huh? Are you there, Nara."

"I... I don't know. Are there two of you, Kari?"

All right, I got it. Her brain had forgotten how to process the two separate sets of optical signals, one coming from each eye. She would have to relearn stereo vision.

"Try closing one of your eyes," I suggested. "That might let you focus on one thing at a time."

She tried it and nodded. "Better. Perhaps we should have added only one at a time. I know it's important to be redundant but—"

"That's it." I heard my voice rise to rather childish squeal but I decided not to care too much. "Nara, you're a genius."

"What? You're going to poke out one of my eyes?"

"No. Thanks to you, we're going to re-program our course and keep us alive."

****

It took several days before I concluded we were on the one unique military ship in the universe where they'd neglected redundancy in the most important part of operations, basic control. It was doubly frustrating after my brag but, no matter where we looked, we could not find a redundant navigation center. It took those days for Nara to adjust to her new eyes and the neural pathways they created. I wondered, though, how could that help? No matter how good her eyesight, she couldn't see what wasn't there.

We all practiced with our military-grade implants. If we were captured, at least we'd give outselves our best shot—which figured to last about five seconds until the slave traders realized what we'd done.

In the meantime, though, we were able move around the ship a little more safely. Anyone getting into trouble could signal for help. I insisted we keep the three-person buddy system anyway and, just in case someone got jumped before they could signal, I also dragged another of the A.I.s out of the cargo hold and had it keep track of all the implant locations. That way, if someone got lost or didn't show up when they were supposed to, we'd know where the girl was and where she'd come from.

We also kept a guard on the dining area and announced over the ship intercom that any sailor left behind who wanted to eat could turn themselves in.

One by one, those sailors Harding and the other officers had deserted when they'd hit the lifepod showed up, hungry and pissed at being captured by a bunch of girls.

Every time I got the call that another had come in, I went down and interviewed them before letting them join their fellows in the former slave pit. I felt certain that one of them would tell me how to interface with the A.I.s that ran the ship's engines. Maybe they could have, but every single one clammed up.

Nara put herself in charge of the pit… even after I explained that she couldn't just space the sailors like they'd tried to do to us.

We'd been traveling for four days ship-time when Ronin woke me.

"Got something for you."

I looked and wished I hadn't. When I'd first tasted it, blood had been disgusting. Then, it had gotten kind of exciting. Lately, it had just gotten boring. Sure, I needed it to keep going, but I didn't get the rush any more ... or maybe I was always living in the rush.

"Drink it," he said. "We've got something to show you and I need you to have all of your capabilities intact."

The 'we' was Ronin and Shena, who still tagged after him like pilot fish.

With that as motivation, I choked down the small cup of blood, then motioned him to get on with it.

"You know how the redundant control center is missing?" he said.

"Look, I'm not a spaceship designer but there should be one." I might have been a little cranky. I was pissed that, after all we'd been through, Shena and the others were still going to end up enslaved.

"It's just," he said, "that Shena and I have been going over the ship schematics."

Shena grinned at Ronin's recognition and breathlessly took over the conversation. "We believed you even when *you* started doubting."

"We searched everywhere," I grumbled. "Maybe the slavers scrapped it when took over the ship. To make more room for cargo"

"Yeah," Shena said. "We couldn't find anything on the schematics but then we thought of how you had the AI tracking everyone on the ship."

"Yeah, for safety."

Ronin called up an image and sent it to me. "The lines represent where any of us has traveled through the ship."

Thin green lines traced the entire interior of our ship—not a huge surprise. The ship was big but everyone had been out the searching for my theoretical but missing redundant control center so the green when almost everywhere.

The green was thickest at the dining hall and around the bathrooms.

I glared at Shena. "After what they've been through, don't you think the crew deserves a little privacy?"

Ronin looked embarrassed but Shena nudged him. "Keep going,"

"We didn't identity-code the pattern," Ronin said. "You see how it's all green? Without directly querying the AI, we can't tell who went where, just that someone went."

It took me a while to figure where Ronin was going with this but since he and Shena were looking at me with big expectant eyes, I knew it was something big. Since he'd started this by mentioning the ship schematics, it didn't take genius to figure they were connected. I called up the ship schematic he'd sent me days before and then added the travel lines as an overlay.

"We've been everywhere but inside the engine compartment. Which would be, hello, a place where we'd get turned into atomic debris. So, what's the problem there?"

Shena kept grinning so I looked more closely. How big was the engine? The void where no green lines crossed seemed too large. "Something is hidden, right? Between the engine and the junior officer quarters."

Ronin laughed, then bumped fists with Shena.

Shena shook her head. "I was right."

"There's a spot nobody's visited right in front of the engine," I said. Somehow none of us went there even though we've made an effort to go everywhere."

"Right," Shena said. "We think we should check it out."

"Yeah, I think so, too."

****

I worried some of the sailors might have holed up there, so I gathered a double-team. Me, Shena and Ronin were Paw One. Paw Two was Nara, who I'd dragged out of the prison area, Cassie and Ursula, a small dark-haired girl who looked closer to eight than her actual age of twelve. Nara carried a long gun. I stuck with my plasma stun-gun. The others brought pistols. I didn't know that we were going to run into trouble but wanted to be sure we could dish it out if we did.

We passed the slave pit as we headed toward the *Princess*'s stern and got a series of jeers and suggestive cat-calls from the crewmen we'd locked there.

I took a few seconds to walk over and inspect the repairs on the wall Harding had taken out in his efforts to kill me. My gesture didn't silence the sailors, but it quieted them down some.

The ship's bots had done a good job replacing the original material. The new wall wasn't as imbued with sweat and stink as the old one had been, but I suspected it would look pretty much the same after a few years. Unfortunately, unless we got the ship under control, Security would be in charge of it again, too.

We headed through a doorway that had seemed to be part of the elevator until we'd figured the design, and down another hallway where we came to what certainly looked like a dead end.

I never would have noticed the false wall if I hadn't been looking at the schematic.

The graphene-diamond bulkhead was weathered to the same gray as the other five walls. The stink was the same—a combination of a century's worth of sailor sweat, urine, and paint ... although I didn't think the maintenance bots had painted these walls in decades.

Even looking closely, it was hard to spot the difference. But when I slid my blade down the corner, the blade sunk into accumulated grease rather than meeting solid diamond or steel.

"Shall we blast it?" Nara asked.

I wondered if I should talk to her about her tendency to look for a violent solution to every problem then decided against it. After all, a lot of the problems we faced probably only had violent solutions ... assuming they had any solutions at all.

Still, we couldn't be certain the wall didn't open to vacuum rather than the missing controls. Instead of blasting, I borrowed Ronin's laser-cutter and sliced a tiny hole through the false wall.

Air puffed out of the hole rather than sucking all of us toward it. That was good news. Better news was, my implants registered that air as stale but non-toxic. All we needed was to come this far and then poison ourselves.

I sent Nara's paw to wrangle up a grapple while putting the same kind of camera-bot I'd used to spot Russart's treasury through the little hole I'd made.

The bot didn't have vampire vision and the only light in whatever was on the other side of the hole came through the hole, from the dim corridor behind me.

"Give it a shot with the plasma rifle," Shena suggested. "That would light things up."

Well, it would. It would also light up any intact A.I.s and murder them.

Instead I sliced off the sleeve of my tunic, used the cutter to set it on fire, and dropped the smoldering rag through the hole ... and wished I hadn't.

The uniforms I saw were from Earth's space fleet a century before. The skeletons figured to be the same era since they were wearing the uniforms.

I projected the tri-d visuals to the center of the hallway where we stood waiting for Nara and watched Ronin and Shena react.

"Eeew. That is so gross." Despite everything, I was glad the young Shena, not the overly mature version, was back.

"Hey, imagine if their memory sticks come loaded with a hundred years' worth of salary." Ronin's mental leap was also about what I should have expected. He still saw sailors as prey and, frankly, a week playing hide-and-seek with those who'd manned the *Princess* made me a lot more sympathetic toward that view.

Nara, coming back with her grapple, also gave the predictable reaction. Her vibro-blade would have cut slaughtered the sailors if they'd been alive and not a tri-d of skeletons. "I think they're past killing," I pointed out.

"If there are vampires, why shouldn't there be zombies?"

I couldn't argue with her logic. Besides, it was better safe than sorry and I would be thanking her about now if we'd been held up by zombie Earthers.

It took a couple of minutes to rig up the grapple but once we did, bringing down the false wall only took a few seconds.

There were four dead sailors behind it—two in officer uniforms and the other two wearing the whites of Earther enlisted men. Although I thought they were actually enlisted women.

Ronin couldn't help himself—he searched their pockets and bags, crowing as he found the kind of small treasures people collect—a metallic-platinum "bug" from Tyr, where living things develop exoskeletons out of biologically purified metals; and a memory stick with some ancient interface he couldn't read but that, he was sure, held a century's worth of pay. The photo-block still held miniature figures of what was labeled as the family back on Earth ... although there were also a couple of hot-looking guys wearing nothing but their smiles—I was betting those weren't family at all.

Nara glared around, daring the skeletons to get up when Ronin knocked them down in his haste to get at their treasures.

Cassie retreated to a corner, her hands making wringing motions in front of her chest. "What are they doing here? What killed them? What if it's some disease that ..."

"That what?" Shena demanded. "That nobody has noticed for a hundred years since they died?"

It wasn't impossible that the Earther ship had landed on some planet with virus-analogues that could destroy human flesh. The galaxy was big and most planets, even planets with native life of their own, had never been explored. Still, zeno-life tended to see human-life as inedible or poisonous. I was betting something a lot more mundane had killed these Earthers.

Ronin knocked over the last of the skeletons, in the process dragging skeletal fingers off of a control stick.

"This is First, Corvette San Francisco." The soprano voice had the weird accent of the Earther, always sounding like she was asking a question even when she was making a statement. "It's been two weeks since the emergency commenced. We were hit and the captain killed during our attempt at breakout. It's been a race between our repair crews and the space-roaches tracking us."

"What are space-roaches?" Shena whispered.

"It's what Earthers call people who live in platforms and ships," Nara whispered back. "We, I mean they, think normal people should live on planets."

I'd never seen the virtue of living at the bottom of a gravity well, and I suspected First, or whatever her name was, had spent most of her life in space rather than on Earth. Still, she and I weren't going to have a rational discussion about it. The voice had been recorded decades before and First wasn't doing any more talking.

"The inhabitants of 3-G-7-H-S-419 claimed to have millions of tons of constructed food-sticks—enough to feed all of Earth for more than a day. Per agreement, we delivered solar generators offering a ten percent improvement in their energy technology as exchange. Corvette San Francisco was assigned to ride herd on the 277th supply fleet delegated to pick up the cargo.

"While orbiting over their base, we were attacked by an organized pirate fleet of at least twenty first-class and dozens of second-class warships. Under orders from Captain Abrams, we fled, hoping to warn Earth of this betrayal. During our escape, we destroyed one capital ship and three secondaries but were badly damaged by return fire. If we're able to ..."

I couldn't make out what came next but First's voice came back a few seconds later.

"The enemy fleet has found us. With our engines only ten percent effective, we'll never be able to outrun them. I'm sealing myself and the remaining crew in the battle-two center in hopes that the enemy will determine the ship is not worth salvaging and will abandon it or that we'll be able to overcome any prize crew.

"This is First." Her voice sounded older, rougher. "Apparently the space-roaches weren't fooled by our attempts to make the ship appear abandoned. They've hit us with some sort of virus-containing gas. Lisa and Markus are dead. My implants have failed. And Addie is coming at me ... what are ..."

We listened for another couple of minutes but heard nothing more.

"Addie must have been a vampire," Cassie pointed out.

And the virus that hit them had to be at least somewhat different from the one that had killed my family. For one thing, my parents hadn't lived long enough to record a message. For another, I'd gone a couple of days before the urge to drink blood had become overwhelming. Of course, in the century since they'd taken this ship, Security would have done more research, made sure that their weapon killed more quickly and left them more time to deal with vampires when they popped up. And then again, I'd been frozen and then hospitalized. Who knew what I would have done if it hadn't been for cryo?

"So," Shena said. "What's a Battle-Two Center?"

"Secondary control center," I said, secure in what I'd learned watching hundreds of hours of tri-ds.

"And you think that's where we are?"

"I sure hope so."

****

The good news was, First and her buddies *hadn't* sabotaged the controls in Battle-Two. They'd been hoping that they'd be overlooked behind their false wall and could regain control of their ship once their enemy had departed. She'd been right about being overlooked ... to the tune of a hundred years. She'd been wrong, dead wrong, about Security abandoning the damaged ship ... and about her chances of surviving long enough to retake control.

So much for the good news. The bad news was, these controls, while intact, still demanded authorization. Which made sense. First, this had been a military ship and the military is famous for being security-conscious. And second, First would have known that her plan was a long shot. She would have locked down the controls to make it harder for the pirates, also known as Security, to take over the ship.

Still, Security *had* managed to take over despite her efforts. If they could do it, I should be able to do the same. I wasn't an Earther but the same people hunting her were hunting me. And I'd also learned something. At least according to First, Earther fleets weren't pirates sent out to steal food from the spacers. They were trading fleets that had been attacked by pirates. Considering that most tri-ds are made by the same spacer companies that had probably organized the pirate attacks, it wasn't a huge surprise that they'd turned Earthers into the bad guys.

Ronin finally finished his ghoulish search of the skeletal remains. "Well? Are we any closer to controlling the Princess?"

I shook my head. "I thought maybe we could find fingerprints and construct finger analogues. But after a hundred years or so, too many of the oils have evaporated.

He nudged one of the skulls with his foot. "Yeah. Their eyeballs seem to have evaporated, too. So, we can't get a retinal scan."

We'd already tried their implants, but implants take energy from their hosts. After a few months, let alone a dozen decades, they'd lost all memory.

"What about voice coding," Shena suggested.

"What about it?" Cassie demanded. "You think you can sound like an Earther?"

"I can try." She turned to face the Battle Two Center. "Ship. This is Captain Shena Lorne, taking control. Please override earlier orders."

I'll give her this much ... it was a pretty good Earth accent. Maybe she'd watched more of those tri-ds than I'd thought.

"Over-ride denied." Okay, the ship was less impressed than I'd been. Still, there was some good news. For the first time, the controls had directly responded to one of us.

"Let me try." Nara put her lips directly in front of what we assumed was the command tube. "Ship, this is Nara Fost of E.A.L. Pursuant to Earth Regulation Twelve, I am taking command in direct suppression of slavery."

Okay, I'd been right about her. E.A.L. was Earth Anti-slavery League—an organization designated as terrorist by every space corporation I'd ever heard of.

"Takeover requires confirmation."

Well, hell. First wasn't going to confirm anything—she'd been dead a hundred years. As for her captain, he'd been dead before her. Unless ...

My implant had automatically recorded First's message.

I played it through again, having my implant break it into phonemes. Then I went to work, reassembling the sounds like putting together a puzzle.

Finally, I touched my hand to the camera-bot, uploading my newly constructed message.

"This is First." The bot spoke with First's voice because it was First's voice—just rearranged. "Earth-corvette San Francisco has been seized by space-roach corporation Security. Over-ride existing space-roach commands. Accept next speaker as designated captain for the duration of the emergency."

Not all the words came directly from First's talk, I'd had to construct some from the basic explosives and fricatives of speech. All in all, I thought I'd done a pretty good job.

Now, if only the Battle Two Center's A.I. thought the same thing.

"Query."

Well, that wasn't the answer I was looking for. I looked at Nara who shrugged, then pointed to her mouth.

I nodded and signaled "go ahead."

She shook her head and pointed at me.

"Me?"

Okay, speaking out loud wasn't exactly my plan. But I'd thought Nara, thanks to her status with Earth's Anti-Slavery League, would jump at the chance at command.

Well, if she wanted it, I could make her first officer and let her do all the commanding she wanted.

"Acknowledged," the A.I. said. "Awaiting orders ... Captain."

Chapter Fourteen

Controlling the Corvette *San Francisco* was a step up from hurtling through space on a *Stellar Princess* still obeying commands left behind by Harding and his Security colleagues. A few hours after I'd become captain, maintenance bots sent at my command by Battle-Two had repaired the main control center ... and flushed out two more crewmen hiding deep in mostly-empty cargo holds.

I didn't waste a lot of time questioning them—if Security had never found the ship's backup control center, it wasn't likely they had a lot to offer.

Instead, I called all the ex-slaves together for a council of war in the restored bridge.

While I waited for Nara and her paw to lock up the Battle Two Center, Cassie went on the attack.

"The only reason you're captain is because you talked first. If I'd talked first, I'd be captain and you'd be doing what I say. So, I think it's only fair that—"

"Give it a rest, Cassie," my sister said. "Kari put together the override, remember? I don't seem to recall you doing anything but whining while this was going on."

"Yeah? Well, you're her sister. Of course you're going to be on her side."

"I'm sure not on your—"

"That's enough." I understood that they needed to blow off steam, but if we ended up playing who's on whose side game, we were all going to lose. A pitched battle for control wouldn't help anyone, either. "The reason I called this meeting is because I'm not going to just give orders. Yes, I can tell the ship where to go but what good does that do? I don't know where we want to be when we get there. You're going to get as much a vote in this as everyone, Cassie. So, stop whining and start thinking."

"What did I miss?" Nara, Ronin and Ursula were breathing hard as they came through the bridge's starboard portal. I suspected that meant someone, meaning my sister, had called them and told them there was a mutiny under way. I was pretty sure they'd be on my side in any fight, but I didn't want to fight the ex-slaves, not even Cassie. I'd come on this crazy voyage to save my sister and the other slaves. Enslaving them again wasn't part of the plan.

"I was telling Kari that she doesn't get to be the boss just because she talked to the ship A.I. first," Cassie reported.

"Yeah, that wouldn't be right," Nara said. "How about she gets to be boss because she saved all of us when we were going to get sucked into space? That work better for you?"

"We were only going to be spaced because we wouldn't surrender and because she is a vampire."

Nara shook her head. I felt like doing the same.

I'd known Cassie would be trouble when I'd given her my place in the airlock. This was poetic justice biting.

And speaking of biting, I was starting to feel the urge. I wondered about the ethics of draining a bit of blood from the sailors. The average ex-slave probably massed forty kilos. The average sailor was closer to a hundred. They had a lot more blood than they really needed.

I realized my mind had wandered far from the discussion when I heard Ronin's voice.

"We're not Earth-navy. Calling our ship the *San Francisco* seems wrong. And calling it the *Stellar Princess* is even more wrong because, let's face it, the princesses it was named after are you, meaning the slaves. The *Princess* was in the business of delivering girls to men rich enough to make them princesses—if you think that princesses exist only to give some rich men perverted fantasies."

"The ship's name," I broke in, "is hardly our key issue. We've got command of the ship's navigation, but we're sitting dead in space. Zero acceleration. Zero hyper-jump. Floating forever in space with a hold full of prisoners just doesn't sound that fun."

"Sounds more fun than being slave to some pervert," Shena said.

"Agreed. But we have other options." I turned to Cassie. "For example, we could take you home."

Her face was a picture. First hope. Then, as she thought through my offer, dejection.

"You know I can't go home." Her chin wobbled.

"Actually," I said, "I know Shena and I can't go home. Security bombed our home, killed our parents, turned me into a vampire. But your family—"

"They sold me."

I tried to wrap my mind around that ... and failed. "Your own family?"

"You don't understand. Plauton is all about farms. If you're one with God, you live on a successful farm. But there's only so much land, only so many farms. Suppose the farms were divided equally among all the children? Every generation, they'd get smaller until they couldn't sustain a family. So, only one child can inherit. A family shows it's living in accord with God's will by adding land, not by dividing it."

"Your own family sold you?" I was repeating myself but I was struggling with what she'd said... and what dividing farms on Plauton had to do with selling a girl to Security.

"Security paid them enough that they could buy down some of the farm's debt. Which meant that my brother could get married to a nice girl who was going to inherit her farm. You see, the farm and family can continue, which shows God's favor."

"You think God *wanted* you to be a slave?"

She looked conflicted on that but finally came up with an answer. "It's natural that those who are stronger would dominate those weaker. The Bible is filled with stories of slaves and their—"

"Maybe," Shena said, "it was God's will that Kari came along and rescued you."

Cassie shook her head. "It doesn't work that way."

"Yeah," Nara said. "Makes sense to believe *Harding* represents God's will because he's a strong male and a jerk. Maybe your God isn't strong enough to work through a fifteen-year-old who is actually nice."

"And I don't need your sarcasm or your blasphemy."

I felt pretty certain that waiting until I turned thirty wasn't the answer, tempting though it might be to throw Cassie in cryo for twenty years and then thaw her out.

"Anyone else have someplace to go?" I looked around at the girls, then at Ronin.

Ursula raised her hand. "I guess my parents would take me back. But, come to think of it, Security would just come and get me again. I was collateral and my parents couldn't repay the loan. So, legally, Security still owns me and my parents would have to hand me over. Uh, never mind about going home."

Ultimately, it turned out that none of us had any place to go. Ronin could go back to Gardenia—we'd paid off what he owed Watton so nobody was looking for him—but nobody was waiting for him, either. As for the girls, Security would scoop up anyone within a week of returning home.

"Okay," I said. "We can't go home. We've got a ship. We've got a lot of food-sticks. We can go anywhere in the galaxy. But we—"

"Except you'll drain us of our blood and then we'll all die," Cassie pointed out.

I'd had the ship's A.I. calculate how much blood I could take without causing massive anemia among the others and I wasn't positive that would be enough. So, Cassie had a point. We couldn't just float among the stars and pig down on food-sticks forever. Not unless they put me in cryo, and I wasn't going to do that while Shena was in danger.

Ursula raised her hand like an old-time student in the tri-ds. "Like you said, we've got a ship. Maybe we could become traders."

It wasn't a bad idea. Visiting different ports, I'd be able to get fresh blood supplies. We would have to be careful where we traded, though. Security would be looking to take their ship back. For that matter, Earth would be looking to take their ship back, too. I didn't think either would be especially grateful to a handful of girls for taking care of it.

"One slight problem," Ronin said. "We don't have anything to trade… except slaves."

Nara wheeled toward Ronin, her hands moving into one of her fighting patterns.

"Stop it," I shouted.

"But he said…"

"He wasn't suggesting we put any of us on the market. Were you, Ronin?"

"I was thinking of the sailors. Although there'd be a much better market for young girls."

"Okay, we're not going to sell anyone," I said. "Slavery is evil, and it doesn't matter whether the slaves are girls or disgusting dirty sailors."

"We have to do something with them," Ronin reminded me. "Nara can't watch them forever."

"Right," I said. "We've got to do something with ourselves, we've got to do something with the sailors who got left behind when Harding jumped ship, and we've got to do something about Harding."

"Now that we have the ship operating," Nara said, "we could hunt down and destroy his lifepod."

Cassie gasped. "That would be piracy."

"We'd never catch him," Ronin said. "Those lifepods are designed to head for home—sort of a one-shot drive. By now, he's back in Gardenia. Probably outfitting a fleet to come looking for us."

I queried the bridge A.I. and learned that Ronin was right about the way lifepods worked. They're designed to go home even if their passengers are too sick to crew them. So, they'd burn out their engines and deliver their cargo.

I suspected he was also right about Harding's intentions. The man would take being defeated by a group of girls as an insult—and do whatever he could to get his revenge.

"It sounds like we can't do anything," Shena said. "We can't just float here because Kari needs fresh blood. We can't go into the merchant business because we don't have any cargo and because wherever we try to trade, Security will grab us. And we can't go home because none of us has a home to go back to."

"There is Cassie's idea," Ronin said.

"Huh?" Cassie looked confused. "What did I say?"

"You said we could go pirate."

****

By warship standards, the *Blood Star*, which, at Ronin's insistence, was the new name for the former *Stellar Princess*, was small and lightly armed. By merchant standards, it was small but deadly. The typical merchant ship is equipped with a couple of single-shot missile launchers and a laser nose cannon. The *Star*, in contrast, had four multiple-shot launchers, a nose-cannon, two stern cannons, and an active anti-missile railgun array. The old Earther navy had definitely produced fighting ships better than anything the space community managed, even a century later. Which was probably one reason Security had kept the *Star* in operation... and quite likely the reason they'd stolen it in the first place.

As I saw it, there were really only three problems. First, if we wanted to be pirates, we'd have to find ships to plunder. Second, we'd have to find someplace safe and reliable where we could sell our loot, take on crew, and buy supplies. Third, we'd have to be ready to fire on merchant ships that refused to heave to on our orders.

I called up the mental image of my parents lying in pools of their own blood and shook my head. I just couldn't kill innocent merchants, even if they were stupid enough to ignore my orders. But I was pretty sure that we'd have to if we went pirate. Merchants don't give up their ships if they aren't absolutely convinced that their alternative is worse. Threats from a fifteen-year-old girl weren't likely to induce the kind of terror a pirate needed to be successful.

Which meant, twelve hours after Ronin had suggested we go pirate, we were still dead in space.

I'd learned one lesson from my first all-hands meeting. I wanted to have an actual plan before bringing the crew together again. So, I had Nara, Shena and Ronin meet with me in Battle-Two.

"Okay," I said. "We've got to dump off the sailors. Because they're taking too much of your time, Nara."

"Not like I've got anything else to do."

"Which brings up our second point. We've got a ship that can run rings around most of the merchants out there and is probably faster than ninety percent of even Security's military vessels. So, we've got to put it to use."

"The E.A.L. has always wanted a ship," Nara said. "We could—"

"From what I've heard," Ronin interrupted, "the Earth Anti-Slavery League could buy any ship they wanted. So, I'm guessing they don't want one *too* badly. Besides, suppose we did go after slavers. The only way we could make any money would be to sell the slaves ourselves. And that sort of defeats the purpose, doesn't it?"

"We're *not* selling slaves," Shena said.

"Well, yeah. But that brings back the question of how we make money. We don't have mining equipment on board. So, we're going to need to buy water, carbon, platinum, other materials that the platforms and planets provide."

"Surely the slaves' families will offer rewards," Nara said. "We could—"

"How big is the reward *your* family offered, Nara" Ronin interrupted. "How about you, Shena? Your parents offering the big bucks? This isn't some fairy tale where we rescue the magical princess and she makes us all rich. Security picks slaves from the poor, from the orphans, from those who can't pay their protection fees. Even if they wanted to, those families wouldn't have the money to keep the *Star* going.

"Being a pirate should be fun," Shena said. "People are supposed to worry about us, tremble in fear over the assault of the Bloody Stars. Plus we get to talk like pirates. Like, 'shiver me timbers.' Instead, we're spending our time worrying about boring things."

"Boring things like keeping the ship spaceworthy," I said. The basic issue remained. We could agree to go after slave-ships, but we couldn't sell their cargo. And Ronin and Nara were the only ones willing to actually attack merchant ships.

"Earth is always buying," Nara reminded us. "We could loot merchant ships of their food and carbon and ship it back to Earth."

"Except the first time they see our ship, they confiscate it," Shena said. "Besides, none of us wants to blow up merchants."

"How about we don't just take the cargo," Nara said, "we take the whole ships. We can ship the whole lot back to Earth and Earth-Fleet never sees the *Blood Star* so they won't know that it used to be Earth forces."

"They wouldn't let us take the ships back," Ronin said, "so we'd lose every prize crew we sent."

I held up my hand. "Hold it, there's something here but I need to process it."

Ronin was right—it didn't matter what we sent toward Earth, they'd grab it and keep it. With its hundreds of billions of people, Earth needed every drop of water, every molecule of carbon, every photon from the sun just to stay even. That was why Earth had sent out its fleets. It was also why Earth had stopped sending the fleets—the costs of maintaining them had gradually exceeded what they could buy or plunder from ever-more-distant spacer colonies.

But it did make sense to grab ships rather than just cargo. Ships always have value. We could sell them ... regardless of their cargo.

"Obviously some of the stories of Earth's fleet are lies," I said. "But not all of them. I never met my grandparents, but my parents told me how a couple of Earth battleships cleaned out Diana. My parents met on an evacuation ship but their parents had to stay behind. The next time ships visited Diana, there was nothing but corpses."

"Scare stories," Nara said.

"They were younger than me when it happened, but my parents were there. Earth pays if they have to, but they take what they need one way or another."

"Well, anyway," she tried again, "they don't do that anymore."

If anything, I suspected they did it more. Earth's population was still growing, but the fundamentalists controlled more and more of it, and so its scientists were limited in what they were allowed to do to help. Earth couldn't build a second fleet because it needed everything just to stay ahead of starvation. And its old fleet had largely gone rogue, fighting to keep itself alive and not sending much back to its former masters—a hundred years of independence will do that.

"What I'm thinking," I said, "is that we go after slave ships."

Ronin shook his head. "We already agreed there's no money there unless we sell the slaves."

"Which we won't do," Shena said.

"Which we won't do. But we don't just take the slaves ..."

"We take the ships." Nara was shouting. "We sell the ships and set the girls free."

"Or add them to our crew if they don't have any place else to go," I said.

Ronin nodded slowly. "It'll be tricky. The corporations won't be happy when they lose their ships. Whoever we sell them to will have to worry about whether they'll run into corporate warships who'd pirate them back. It's not like cargo—you just change the markers and nobody asks questions. Ships ..." he trailed off.

I got where he was coming from. Dealing in ships would be hard, dangerous for both seller and buyer. Still, there were never enough ships. Colonies got cut off and died because their financers couldn't find a ship to take them vital medical technology. Perfectly functional orbital platforms were abandoned because not enough ships called them home. There had to be people who would pay plenty for a ship ... and who wouldn't ask too many questions about where they came from. People willing to bend the rules, alter registration information, make an old ship look new. The trick, as I saw it, was finding those people.

Chapter Fifteen

"Drive signature detected." The ship's A.I. spoke in First's Earth-accented soprano.

"Announce battle stations," I said.

Across *Blood Star*, chimes called the girls to their posts.

I'd slaved the ship's bridge A.I. to my heads-up, so I watched the indicators go green one by one as each girl reported into her assigned station.

"The girls are complaining," Nara whispered from her post in the Battle Secondary Center. "Too many false alarms, too much running and waiting."

I could understand that. During the first twenty standard days, we'd found four slave ships, freed their slaves, dumped the sailors in the lifepods, and moved on. Now, those four ships orbited a planetless star, their drives shut down, their emissions on minimum. And we'd swelled our crew with the ex-slaves we'd rescued to the point where we had at least one girl at each of the ship's stations.

But that had been the first twenty days. For the next thirty, we'd come across the occasional freighter, but nothing worth capturing. I would have liked to believe that we'd driven slaving out of business but we'd broken some of Security's encryption and learned that Security alone had thirty vessels shipping slaves and the other corporations had plenty more.

We hadn't driven them out of business, they'd simply gotten better at avoiding our probes—which wasn't a complete surprise considering that Security had owned the *Blood Star* for the better part of a century. They had to know its capabilities ... and limitations ... a lot better than any of us.

Now, though, somebody had slipped.

"You think it's another merchant?" Shena brushed her thumb against the manual firing key.

"It's moving fast and it's trying to hide its drive signature in that bright star," I said. "And its heat profile is more like the slavers we found than the merchants. Living cargo and extra crews generate infrared emissions that frozen cargo doesn't."

"This'll be five ships we've captured," Shena gloated. "That's a fleet. Maybe we shouldn't sell them at all. Maybe we should arm them and—"

"They must have spotted us." Nara's voice cracked. She was pure cool when it came to fighting with her hands. Not so much when she fought ships. "She's running."

"Drop cloaking," I ordered. "Accelerate to full speed."

Blood Star throbbed and the artificial gravity—which we'd reduced to a more comfortable twenty percent of Earth-normal, pulsed off as we diverted power to the drives.

From around the ship, I heard scattered shrieks—not everyone had followed training and strapped themselves down.

I'd hoped to be able to get a lot closer before the slaver spotted us. A stern chase is no fun, especially since the ship we pursued could dump mines or big blocks of iron in our path—running into those on full acceleration could end our anti-slavery ambitions in a hurry.

The slaver was fast.

Since taking over *Blood Star*, I'd let the repair bots run all over the engines and control room and carved off an ugly bolted-on section of cargo bays that must have accumulated over the decades as Security turned the ship from a warship into something that could haul freight as well as slaves. After dumping all that mass, I was pretty sure the *Star* was faster than it had been at least since it had been Earth-Fleet. Which meant, it should be faster than Security would expect. But the slaver we were chasing was fast, too. Could they get away?

Finally, though, the sensors ticked ... we were gaining.

An hour later, we were appreciably closer.

"Signal them," I told Ronin. "Tell them that their officers and crews will be released unharmed if they surrender."

Ronin got on the whisper-laser and, I assume, fired off the message. At this distance, it would take at least a couple of minutes before we'd get an answer ... if they were listening and chose to answer at all.

I was still counting down the seconds of light-latency when the slaver flared up on our sensor displays.

"What the heck?" Shena demanded.

I'd feel bad if it blew itself up trying to get away from me. Not *too* bad, though, I tried to persuade myself. A quick death was better than what slaves would get if they were delivered. And besides, it wasn't me who'd shipped them into slavery—I wasn't putting that on my conscience.

I only realized how badly I'd been lying to myself when I saw that the slaver was intact and still accelerating ... but doing so more slowly.

"Must have lost an engine," Ronin reported. "The A.I. reports that the radiation is consistent with a tokamak collapse."

Instead of gaining by tiny increments, suddenly we were overhauling them in huge chunks of distance.

"Sweet," Shena said. "What luck they blew an engine just when we were chasing them."

"Probably overloaded it trying to get away," Ronin said. "Word is out on what we were doing."

Word was out, yet this ship had walked into our reach. Maybe this was too easy.

"Can our scanners detect anything about the ship?" I asked.

"Other than it's not as fast as it used to be?" Ronin snickered as he targeted the distant ship with his lasers. They couldn't do any damage at this distance but their reflections would serve as active sensors, providing better detail than we got from the passives already in place.

"Reduce to three-quarter acceleration," I said.

"Confirmed," the ship's soprano said. "Acceleration at three quarters full."

"Hey, we were catching them," Shena said.

"Yeah, and we were going to fly right by them. We need to capture them, right, not blow them up as we rush past."

"It's sort of funny, though," Ronin mused.

"Huh? What's that?"

"You'd think they'd be throwing stuff at us. I mean, we're right behind them."

"Maybe they haven't thought of that," I said. "I mean, what are the odds that we end up on a pure stern chase."

"Why wouldn't we?" Shena asked. "If somebody was coming after me, I'd turn and run the other way."

"Right." My sense of danger picked up. "But you're a relatively small mass and you can actually turn. Spaceships don't work that way. They have momentum and need to accelerate to brake that momentum. The only way they could be going dead away from us is—"

"If they put themselves that way on purpose," Ronin concluded.

"Change course," I said. "sixty degrees relative to current heading. Twenty-five degrees Z-axis. Full speed nominal."

The ship's engines whined and the images in the display shifted as we changed our vector. We were still heading in the general direction of the slaver but not straight for it. Which meant, we could still go after it if that made sense, but we'd no longer be in its direct path.

"What the heck," Nara called from Battle Secondary Control. "We had them and you're giving them a chance to get... uh-oh. What are those?"

Those were six new displays that lit up just about when sensors at those distances would have observed our course change.

"Looks like Security got tired of losing slave ships and set an ambush." I should have recognized the situation earlier but I wasn't a trained space fighter. I'd had a few weeks with ship A.I. but a real captain would have trained for years, not days.

"Analyze bogie position and best-guess their plans," I told the A.I.

A.I.s can sometimes take forever to analyze human activities. In this case, though, the display was up in a fraction of a second... and showed the half-dozen ships, plus the slaver we'd been chasing, all converging on a spot not too far from where we'd been heading.

"Probability is eighty-seven percent that this was the original plan," the A.I. said in First's soprano. "Variance as follows." The first display showed the ships' arcs in blue. The second, in red, showed us on our new trajectory. The good news was, we'd outrun

143

three of the seven. The bad news was that the other four would chew us up.

"I've got a positive I.D. on five of them," Nara reported from Battle Secondary. "All Security."

"We've got to surrender." Cassie's station was the sick bay, which would have kept her off the battle network under normal conditions. Apparently she'd thought the situation bad enough that she needed to override.

"You know what they do to pirates," Ronin fired back. "And don't think your defeatism means they wouldn't let the eater nanobes get you, too."

I shuddered. I'd never forget the video of nanobe eaters digesting a living pirate that Security had broadcast to every tri-d system on Mjolnir. The microscopic things started very slowly, self-replicating until they could digest a living human in big gulps… while the pirate screamed.

"That isn't happening." I thumbed the 'all stations' indicator. "Okay, guys. We've got multiple Security pirates who want to shut down our anti-slavery game. We're going to be doing some tricky maneuvers so if you're not strapped down yet, you've got about five seconds to make it happen. Gunners, you've had it easy up 'til now, just firing across bows to make unarmed slavers stop. Well, guess what? This time it's for real."

Ronin, Shena and I gamed ship A.I. for a few minutes. The Security ships had us truly boxed in, but space is big… and it's a lot harder to spring a trap in three dimensions than in the two dimensions of a playground. I was betting that Security's captains didn't have a whole lot more experience at this kind of tactic than I had … although they'd probably been planning it for weeks now. Since Earth-fleet had stopped its raids, there hadn't been much need for fleet-style actions by the corporations.

"Prepare for acceleration." While the alarms wailed I waited three seconds to make sure everyone had a chance to strap in, then hit it. "Flank speed. Starboard gunners, fire when your weapons bear. Rail gunners, please do better than you did in our last drill."

I drove the *Star* down the throat of the nearest Security ship. No way could we avoid them all, but they'd planned on boxing us in, gang up on us like a swarm of honey-grunts over a pig. By heading straight for one of them, I hoped to reduce the battle to a one-on-one match. Since they were heading for us, if we survived the conflict, this ship would be way out of range before they could turn around and come after us.

The ship whined and the lights dimmed as we hit flank speed acceleration. We couldn't maintain this speed... it would tear the ship apart, but I figured getting hit by Security's missiles would do more damage.

"Bogey one has flared up its supposedly defective engine," Shena reported. "You were right in suspecting a trap."

If I'd been so right, why had I walked into it?

"Let's worry about bogie two," I said.

The *Star* jolted. "Missile two launched. Missile one launched. Missile three launched." The reports tripped over each other.

"Reload," I said. "I want to hit them again."

"We're down to only a couple more," Shena reminded me.

"Not like we can save them for another fight if we lose this one."

The Security ship changed vectors but I adjusted ours to match. Fewer of our weapons could bear that way, but they had the same problem... and any Security ships behind us had to be careful not to hit their ally while aiming at us.

Missiles don't have to hit their target to do damage. Like old-time depth charges, they explode when they reach proximity. The expanding mass of plasma turns both the fragmentation material of the missiles themselves (generally iron) and the target ship (generally carbon) into shrapnel.

At least that's the theory.

The outgas cloud from bogie two said that the theory had worked well enough.

"Reduce to full speed," I commanded as we shot past bogie two.

Once we were past the intercept, we had a stern chase of our own.

I had Nara, in Battle Station Two, toss out one-ton blocks of stealthed ferro-carbon. I didn't think we'd actually hit anything, but nobody wants to run into a big radar-evading mass. When they figured they were out there, Security's ships would have to slow.

****

Twenty-three course changes, five days, and a dozen translations later we were back in orbit with our captured ships … and Security was nowhere to be seen.

I looked around the bridge. Shena had fallen asleep with her mouth open, drooling on a data stick. Ronin looked out on his feet but he was still awake. *Star*'s A.I. reported the change in status as our crew stood down from their action stations and returned to normal readiness.

"Home sweet home," I said. "That was a disaster."

"We survived," Ronin said as I matched orbit with one of our prizes.

"Yeah," I said. "Lucky us."

"We could have gotten killed. If you hadn't guessed something was wrong, we would have been in the middle of their trap rather than at the edge."

"Look, Ronin. I appreciate you trying to cheer me up but our goal here isn't just to stay alive. Every day dozens, maybe hundreds of girls get taken from their families and turned over to perverts. And right now, we're doing exactly nothing to help them."

"Hey," Ronin said, "there's a big anti-slavery league, right? They've got what, billions of members with a newsletter and dues and politicians. How many slave ships have they captured in the past couple of months? Zero is the answer. And there are what, fifty of us now, counting the girls we freed who don't know anything about running a ship. But we captured five, and then when Security sprung a trap on us, we escaped, damaging one of their ships in the process. I'd say we have a lot to be proud of."

"Fine. But that's history. All of that was in the first couple of weeks. Now, they've gotten smarter and we're not catching anything … we're just trying to avoid being caught ourselves."

He shrugged. "Before I ran into you I spent a year in the worst alleys in Gardenia. Every day could be the day I ran out of luck, the day Security found me or one of the crime lords decided I'd broken too many rules. I learned to take each day as a gift and that's still the way I feel. So boo-hoo if someday something bad is going to happen to us. In the meantime, we're going to do what we do, free some more slaves, take the slave traders' ships from them, and make the slave traders' and owners' lives miserable."

I opened my mouth to argue but couldn't. He might be wrong about himself, but he was exactly right when it came to me. Vampires were everyone's enemy. They were hunted, killed like vermin. And pirates were on the next step near the bottom of the food chain. Which meant that the Security trap we'd evaded was just the start. They'd keep gunning for us. Sooner or later we'd take the wrong chance, attack the wrong ship. Sooner or later, they'd get us. And when that happened, we'd be lucky if they just blew our ship up because what they'd do to any young girl pirates they captured didn't bear thinking of.

So, every day *was* a gift and I certainly didn't have anything better to do with those gifts than to make life miserable for the perverts who controlled the space corporations while, at the same time, perhaps freeing a few teens who'd gotten swept up in their profitable scams. It wasn't a bad life for a vampire. That didn't make it a life I wanted for my sister or for the other members of the crew.

I'd promised myself I wouldn't hold another all-hands meeting until I knew what I wanted out of it. But I hosted this one anyway.

Chapter Sixteen

"I don't know how much we'll get for the ships we captured," I told the group. "But whatever it is, we'll split it in two halves. One goes to the *Star*—we need it for refueling and resupplying. The second we'll divide in equal shares for each crewmember, based on whether you were on crew when we took that ship. If you want, you can leave. It probably won't be enough to set you up in luxury, but it should be something. Ronin and I are going to stay with the *Star*—there isn't anyplace else for us to go. Any of you who want to stay can ... but think about this. What happened with that Security trap wasn't just a coincidence. They set it up and we walked into it. As long as we're out here, they'll be hunting for us."

"As long as we're out here," Shena said, "they'll be spending their money trying to find us, which means they make less money from their slave trade."

"*You* aren't going to be out here," I said. "You're going to—"

"To what?" she interrupted. "Am I going to buy myself a new family? Maybe I can find some nice pervert who'll take me in free... no need even to spend money on a slave. You're the only family I have left, Kari, and I'm not going to leave you."

"There is one other option." Nara looked around at the other girls. "Earth doesn't allow slavery. And I'm sure they'd be grateful for the return of this ship."

I forced myself to stay silent. Maybe Earth would be grateful for the return of one small remainder of its once-vast fleet.

"Earth can't feed itself," Ronin said. "That's why they built the fleet in the first place. A dozen decades later, it's gotten worse. Yeah, maybe they'd take us but what could we do there? It's not like they need more people."

"I don't want to go to Earth," Cassie said. "Everyone knows people there are just stacked on top of each other. They can't do anything but watch tri-ds because there's no room. Besides, if we give them back the *Star*, they'll probably use it to be real pirates... and they won't bother with helping the slaves."

"Uh, what do you care?" Shena demanded. "You didn't want to do any of this."

"Doesn't mean I want Earthers to pirate. I mean, they might raid Plauton where my parents and brother are. We'd never do that."

"Any other thoughts?" I asked.

The discussion went on but no light was shed. Of the hundred and fifty ex-slaves we now had in our crew, seven wanted to take the money and make new lives for themselves. The rest, including Cassie, signed on for another stint.

"Okay," I said about half an hour after I'd realized nothing was getting said. "Nara, Ronin and I will see what kind of price we can get for our prizes. Then we'll return and hand out the money. If anyone decides they don't want to stay and pirate, they can change their minds then."

"Assuming you come back," Cassie said.

"What's that supposed to mean?"

"Hello. They know who you are. They're hunting for you in space but they've got to know we need to find a market for our prizes. If you walk into some port and offer a bunch of spaceships for sale, you don't think Security will grab you in a hurry?"

I'd been so ready to take offense that I'd practically bit her head off when she was simply pointing out the dangers. "That's why I'm taking Ronin," I said. "He knows the crooks and creeps."

"What about Nara?"

"So she can kill them."

Cassie nodded. "There are plenty of people out there who need killing."

She was right. Unfortunately, if our plan had a chance to work, we'd have to do business with some of those who needed killing most of all.

****

The largest of the ships we'd captured had a launch equipped with a star-drive. Compared to the *Blood Star*, it was slow. But it wouldn't be as recognizable as would one of the full-sized ships, and it could land just about anywhere.

We set down near a mine about fifty kilometers outside of Gardenia. Then Shena, Cassie and Ursula took off, leaving us to make our way to the town.

A few minutes later, a couple of Security fighters flew over. No big surprise—everyone had to know that we'd need to make contact to unload our cargo, and the only contacts we had were in Gardenia. Still, it served as a warning—Security was watching.

Our drop-off point was on the opposite side of Gardenia from our lab, but it had once been the biggest mine on Mjolnir. My mother had once brought me here to learn to navigate various types of caverns and passageways, since it had just about every sort.

Most of the planetoid's mining had been for water. A thin seam, though, presumably laid down by a nearby supernova, had consisted of semi-stable transuranics, and had been mined intensively. Semi-stable transuranics were sort of like the gold rushes of a thousand years before back on Earth… and miners had hunted up every scrap.

The mined-out seam had headed toward Gardenia, and we went underground.

I wasn't exactly getting used to being a vampire—having to go to my crew and beg them for a few sips of blood every day served as a constant reminder of how different I was. Still, I had gotten used to my ability to see using only the infrared light cast by rocks heated by the distant Asgard and by constant twisting caused by the gravitational pull of the much nearer Thor working on the inevitable weaknesses caused by massive mining of the planetoid's interior. Between that and residual radiation, the seam might as well have been floodlit—for me, that it.

The others weren't vampires, though, and I'd been concerned about how they'd do.

Nara navigated in the darkness better than I would have guessed. Months of blindness had given her a sense of what surrounded her that didn't depend on visible light. As for Ronin, he kept a grip on my belt and I made sure to stop every few minutes and provide a bit of light so he wouldn't panic. It might have been safe, and it certainly would have been quicker, for us to light up our path the whole way. Our near-disaster with Security's trap made me cautious.

The old mine schematics I'd been working from showed the ore seam tailing out about a meter below the planetoid's surface almost directly outside Gardenia, but I wasn't completely surprised at the cave-in about a kilometer before the supposed end of the trail. The miners hadn't wasted money shoring up the caves, and Thor's tidal pressures were immense.

We'd brought shaped dimensional explosives contemplating exactly this eventuality, but I thought I saw a glimmer of color and had Nara and Ronin help me move some of the accumulated rock pile.

Sure enough, we dug and scrambled our way out of one of Mjolnir's many sinkholes.

As always, Thor hung overhead covering a quarter of the sky like a huge balloon shedding its cool reflective light while mostly protecting us from the glare and destructive rays of Asgard, the star.

My implants chimed connectivity—we were in range of Gardenia's network and no longer dependent on implant-to-implant direct communication.

Ronin cocked his head in obvious response to getting a similar message. "We could call Watton. He'd have a way of bringing us in."

I'd thought about that—entering Gardenia with Security on alert would be dangerous for us. Leaving was likely to be even more problematic. But calling ahead begged for betrayal. After all, the people we planned to meet were criminals and smugglers—most of them would sell their best friends for Security's rewards.

Walking up to the gates of Gardenia and asking to be let in would set off alarms in every Security office in the platform. Harding knew about me and Nara for sure. I suspected he had fingered Ronin as well.

The ancient airlock Ronin and I had used before, though, had seemed safe. So, I planned on taking the same route in we had last time.

****

"You're being paranoid." Ronin was getting impatient after we'd huddled just inside the broken dome for the better part of an hour. Well, I was getting impatient, too.

"Another fifteen minutes," I signed back

Even through his rebreather helmet, I couldn't miss his sigh. "There's no way they know about the airlock. It's been here forever and they've never nabbed a smuggler using it."

"I'm sure they know all the ways in—and they just don't bother with minor smuggling operations."

He shook his head, but I insisted on waiting.

My implant timer finally counted down the last seconds and chimed. "All right," I signed. "I guess we can—" then I grabbed Ronin's arm and yanked him back.

Something about that shadow ... I narrowed my focus and scanned in. Hell, I'd been right. "Security bot. Let's get out of here ... carefully."

We made our way away from the tunnel, keeping our heads down and moving in irregular spurts, hoping that would confuse any pattern recognition program that might be looking our way.

"We're a kilometer from safety and we can't get in," Ronin griped. "What are we going to do?"

I wondered if I was turning into my mother, because I'd been considering alternatives since we captured Blood Star. "Who goes in and out of Gardenia all the time because nobody would dare get in their way?"

"Security," Nara guessed.

"Yeah, them. But they would recognize each other and there's no way we could pass."

It was hard to tell beneath the rebreather mask but Ronin looked excited. "You mean—"

"Yeah, spacers."

Big ships orbit, rather than landing at the spaceport. Mjolnir didn't have a lot of gravity, but the monster-freighters have a lot of mass. One slight miscalculation and Gardenia's dome would shatter. If that happened, everyone inside would cough their lungs out into the vacuum. So, most ships sent down launches with crew and self-propelled containers with cargo.

We'd just have to figure a way to blend in.

****

152

Unlike the first time I'd wandered around Mjolnir with Ronin, this time I had a rebreather I could trust. I'd filled its cartridges with fresh chemicals myself.

Still, after twelve hours waiting outside the spaceport, I was happy when a launch settled down on the glassine landing area and a dozen sailors piled out.

"We could take them," Nara said. "But I'm not sure we could do it without one of them getting a call out."

"If we'd brought sniper-rails," Ronin, ever-bloodthirsty said, "we could—"

I squinted and my vampire-vision zoomed in to the launch. Painted in big white letters against the carbon-black skin, the boat proclaimed itself the property of the *Bartered Princess*. If that didn't sound like a slave-ship, I didn't know what would.

"They'll split up." Too often, I based my beliefs on what I'd seen in the tri-ds rather than real-life experience, and this was one of those times. Still, what were the odds that a dozen sailors would want to spend more time with each other after having no other company for the months of space voyage? They'd better split up. I didn't want to wait for another ship and taking out slavers sounded like a good plan.

For once, the tri-ds came through. Minutes after they'd disembarked, four of the sailors headed for a landing-zone bar while the others proceeded toward Gardenia.

"The ones at the bar are the target," I signed.

We made our way toward the bar. "I'm going in," I told the others. "Wait here."

"What if you get in trouble?" Nara asked.

"If I'm not out in half an hour, you can come in and rescue what's left of me. If they drag me out, you can take them right away."

"Why don't you just wait here with us?" Ronin asked rationally. "They'll be heading for town when they're through."

"I want to make sure of it."

I stepped into the bar's airlock and cycled through.

The bar was cleaner than Watton's place. The bottles on the shelves showed labels I didn't recognize ... some marked in characters that I couldn't read. That didn't mean they actually contained what they promised, of course.

The bartender glanced at me and then shot a thumb at a grizzled oldster who lumbered to his feet and headed toward me. I probably looked like a local grifter to him and he'd want his cut.

I skipped over to the four sailors. "Hey guys. Buy a girl a drink before the bouncer tosses me out."

One of the sailors spat at my feet. Another, though, tossed a cash-chip on the bar. "A soda for the little one. Make it a good one, know what I mean."

He must have watched some of the same tri-ds I had because everyone in the joint knew what he meant ... dope the soda with something to make me go to sleep. I'd wake up in the hold of the slave ship ... and he'd have a nice bonus as well as whatever fun he wanted with a sleeping girl.

I pulled my breathing mask up but didn't take it off—if things went right, I was going to need it. "Thanks, sailor," I said when the bouncer shrugged and stumbled back to his seat in the corner. "You guys have a good voyage?"

The spitter hocked again and I jumped to make sure I didn't get hit. "Waste of time jumping all over the galaxy to avoid some supposed pirates. Like anyone is going to attack us."

"Really?" I squeaked. "Pirates?"

"That's the rumor."

"Speaking of pirates," I said, "there are a lot of thieves in Gardenia. Want me to show you around? I know the places you can get good drinks, places you can find the prettiest girls if you want to dance or party, if you know what I mean. Or maybe you like ..."

"Drink up, girlie." The bartender delivered my drink and collected the cash-chip.

"I'll take you around and keep you safe." I pretended to swallow a big gulp but spit most of the soda back into the glass, holding just enough to let my suped-up implant analyze it.

Sure enough, the bartender had slipped me a high-potency, fast-acting soporific.

My implant went to work overtime dealing with the little bit that instantly numbed my tongue and cheeks. After waiting another five seconds, I collapsed into what I hoped was a convincing semblance of unconsciousness.

It was hard to suppress my trained reflex to slap the ground when I hit—but a drugged girl showing martial arts training would send the wrong message.

"Damn, that's good stuff," the spitter said.

"Yeah, let's dump her in the launch and head for town." The man who'd paid for my drink chuckled and, from the clunk I heard, dropped another money-chip on the bar. "With the bonus, we'll be able to hit some sweeter parts of this dump than we managed last time we were here."

He swung me over his shoulder and headed for the airlock.

"Don't you want to cover her head?" the bartender shouted. "It's vacuum out there."

"So she loses a few brain cells," spitter said. "Nobody pays for smarts."

I was starting not to like these guys.

I exhaled as the airlock pumped its air back into the bar so my lungs wouldn't explode. Then, when the exterior door opened, I twisted my head and bit right into the sailor's armpit.

Even in the vacuum, the blood tasted good.

I couldn't hear his scream, of course. Sound doesn't travel in a vacuum. But I sure felt it as he tried to throw me away while I held on with my teeth.

By that time, Nara and Ronin were mixing it up. Nara did her slow-motion magic while Ronin used a little blade-cutter to slice rebreather hoses. Once the hoses were cut, the sailors lost interest in fighting—or noticing the vampire-girl knocking them on their heads with a rock.

Thirty seconds after the airlock opened, I'd had a couple of good swallows of blood, and we had four unconscious sailors.

"Got to patch up their hoses," I signed as I adjusted my own rebreather.

"Why?" Ronin demanded. "They're slavers. Let them die."

"Because I'm an idiot. Humor me, okay?"

I picked the three smallest, scanned their implants and then over-wrote our IDs with their codes. Once again the military-grade implant upgrade was paying off. Earth navy technology even from a century before was better than made it out to the sticks.

While I was doing that, Ronin and Nara patched the sailors' rebreathers and dragged the unconscious jerks to an abandoned freight container.

We glued them inside with the epoxy we'd brought to build our ladder out of and I checked to see how long they'd last.

A fully charged rebreather system should last for a week. But these guys hadn't planned on extended walks in vacuum. Three of them were good for a couple of days. The fourth had a bare twenty-four hours.

We wouldn't have anywhere nearly that long before they woke up, called for help, and Security was all over Gardenia looking for us.

The smart plan was to kill them. But I just couldn't make myself do it.

"Thump them all one more time on their heads with the eraser," I told Nara. "If one of them resets and starts making calls before we're inside, we're dead."

Then, using the sailors' codes, we walked straight through one of Gardenia's main airlocks.

Chapter Seventeen

"You've got a lot of nerve coming here." Watton glared at the three of us paying special attention to Ronin. "Security is going nuts. If you were going to attack some sailors, why couldn't you just kill them and lose their bodies?"

"You moved some merchandise for us a few months ago," I said. "We've got more."

"Yeah, you owe me for that. Security came down on me hard for unlicensed Hasro. I had to pay off—"

"You seem like an intelligent man," I lied. "I'm sure you took that into account when you made the deal. This deal, though, is bigger—big enough to make everyone rich."

Watton's snarl said he wasn't used to getting interrupted. "I've still got half your stash," he said. "Won't need more for months."

"We aren't talking about a few kilos of Hasro this time," I said. "We're talking about something big."

"Big for a couple of kids is not big for me?" He still looked grumpy, but he looked interested, too.

"Big for anyone. Tens of millions."

"Nothing worth that much. Hell, unless you're talking ships or something there's ..." he jumped as if he'd touched an electrical current. "You're in with the pirates?"

"You heard about that?"

"Everyone's heard about it. Security has offered a million for capture of the pirates and return of the stolen ships."

"Pretty cheap," I said. "I figure they're worth a hundred million."

"Each," Nara put in.

"Ships are ..." Watton wiped sweat off his forehead. "I don't deal in that."

"You didn't deal in Hasro," I reminded him. "But you made a nice commission. I figure you can do a lot better out of this."

"Well ..."

I could almost see the wheels in his brain working. He could deal with us. He could turn us over to Security and get a reward.

Or he could try to take us over and keep all the money for himself. I was pretty sure greed would win, which meant he'd play along with us ... and make the contacts he needed to sell the ships. Getting the money he promised us would be the trick. Spacer chips worked fine when dealing with a few thousand bucks. But nobody spends hundreds of millions in spacer chips. We needed an account, something that looked like a legitimate business.

No wonder those old-time pirates in the tri-ds went around burying treasure everywhere. The money laundering angle was hard.

"The thing is," I said, "we have several ships to unload. And we're planning on getting more. We're looking for a long-term partner. If that's not you, let us know. We can still float you a finder's fee better than Security's lousy million."

He glanced toward the door, then back at me. "You've grown up since you were here last."

"You know, Watton, this really isn't about me right now. It's about you. You've got your little business here, abusing a few women, loan-sharking a few people, breaking some kneecaps and trying to keep your nose clear of Security while eating their leavings like a scavenger fish following a shark."

"I'm no scavenger." He snarled at me, showing me artificially extended canines.

When he'd offered me blood before, I'd assumed he was a vampire like me. I didn't have any kind of vamp-dar, but all of a sudden, I didn't think so. He was too obvious. He was a vampire wanna-be.

I could use that.

I stood. "Come on, guys. Watton, you can use that dead letter drop we set up if you want to contact us. You dealt with us fairly last time so we figured we'd give you first shot. But clearly—"

He glanced at the door again, then reached out to grab my arm. "Sit. I never said we couldn't—"

I pressed my hand down on his so he couldn't release his grip, stepped back and pivoted my body, stretching out his grip and turning up his elbow.

He tried to jerk away but I brought my free hand, palm down, into his elbow not quite hard enough to break, but hard enough to cause some pain. I'd learned my lesson from the fight in the slave pit. Striking too softly wasn't going to be my problem anymore.

"Oww. What do you think—"

"Here I thought we were negotiating, not backstabbing. I suggest you show us your secret way out."

"But—"

I twisted harder. Watton was a huge man and I was small for my age. But I had the leverage. If he tried to use his strength, he was welcome to tear his elbow apart and separate his shoulder. I'd still drive him into the ground.

"Hit him," I told Nara.

She knew what I meant and popped him with the implant eraser. Nobody wanted him making any calls.

Ronin took out his sawed-off scatter-gun and pointed it at the bartender who looked like he might want to involve himself.

"Huh?" Watton looked confused by the sudden loss of his implant.

"Hit the bartender, too," I told Nara.

"Now, Watton," I continued while Nara went about her business. "You and I both know that you have a trap-door out of here. Because we both know you're a tough businessman and no tough businessman is going to let Security seal off the only door in the place. Speaking of which, bolt it, Ronin."

Ronin slid the heavy bar down, closing the front door. The extruded silicates that formed the walls of Watton's bar wouldn't stand up to a determined assault, but I figured the reinforced door was now the strongest part of the place ... and it was where Security would start first.

"What—"

"Don't play dumb." I pressed a thumb into the bundle of nerves at the base of his armpit. "You sold us out for the reward. But guess what?" I jammed my thumb in deeper, letting the nail penetrate skin and licked my lips at the sight of his red blood. "There isn't going to be any reward. First, you won't be alive to get it." I bent closer and took a slurp of the glorious blood. "Second," I said as I pulled away and jerked his arm, separating his shoulder. "Second, we're not getting caught. And third, you're an idiot. They'll kill you rather than pay you whether you deliver us or not."

His scream reminded me of Cassie ... except she at least had the excuse of being a young girl far away from home.

"Okay." Tears ran down his face. "In the kitchen. One of the refrigerators is a false front."

We were halfway into the kitchen when my vampire hearing picked up the sound of someone trying the door ... and discovering it was bolted.

"We're cutting this a little close," I said. "So, here's new deal. We get out and I'm going to forget this ever happened. We'll still do a deal with you, you'll still get rich. But if there are traps, if there are any little accidents, if anything happens, I cut off pieces of you and suck out the blood."

"Turn the refrigerator door handle ninety degrees to the left before you pull on it," he gasped.

"Smart decision." I nodded to Nara. "At least I hope it's a smart decision ... for your sake."

"I swear," he said.

Nara pushed the bartender between her and the refrigerator and turned the handle.

I watched both Watton and the bartender, looking for clues they were trying something.

The small packages behind the refrigerator said that I'd been right about Watton trapping his way out. That it didn't explode said he'd decided not to make the ultimate sacrifice for Security.

"Set the cutters," I told Ronin as Nara hustled the bartender into the passageway revealed behind the false refrigerator. "Let's give Security a surprise."

As if on cue, an amplifed voice shook the bar. "Kari, we know you're in there. Surrender now and we're prepared to be merciful."

"Guess Harding made it back safe and sound," I said.

Ronin finished placing the explosives we'd brought when we'd thought we would have to cut our way out of the mine shaft, and the five of us, including Watton and his bartender, made our way down into Watton's escape route.

"Now," I said. "Let's head someplace comfortable and do some dealing."

The explosion came right after that.

****

I'd hoped we'd catch Harding in the explosion, especially when I learned that he'd been behind the trap that almost caught us. He seemed to be everywhere, and never in a good way.

No such luck, of course. But we did put a couple of dozen Security types in the hospital.

A couple of months before, I would have been horrified that I'd hurt so many. Maybe I was getting hard, maybe being a vampire was changing me, and maybe I'd just seen things fifteen-year-old girls aren't meant to see. Whatever it was, all I could think was that more than twenty trained men wouldn't be hunting me for a while. Maybe one or two of them might even wake up and realize that teenage girls aren't always easy victims. That seemed a stretch, though.

We came out of Watton's tunnel in an abandoned shop, then hired a rent-by-the-hour bed-site from a spaceport bar—one with a non-networked bot attendant so we didn't have to answer any questions.

"I don't trust you," I told Watton when we'd settled down on the thin padding that served as a bed. "Which isn't a problem for me. It is a problem for you, though."

"Look," he said. "This is bull—"

"The problem, you see, is that you don't seem to get that we're your only hope. Security isn't giving you any rewards. They're gunning for you now, same as they are for us. You called them in with a big promise and then sprung a trap on them when they came. No way are you explaining your way out of that cluster. Thing is, I'm not sure you're smart enough to realize that the only way you get a win is to throw in with us completely."

"But—"

"We need a ground-side agent. We need someone to sell our captured ships. We need someone to buy us transuranics for our missiles and anti-matter for our engines. In return, we make that ground-side agent rich. You've got the contacts, which is why we came to you, but there are others and we can find them. The thing is, we need somebody smart. Somebody who can get good prices because he gets a cut and high prices means a bigger cut. Someone who can get us quality components because they'll keep us alive, which means he gets richer. After that boneheaded move of calling Security, I have my doubts you're the right man. So, maybe we just kill you and move on. Hell, what's your bartender's name. Maybe he's got the balls to—"

"I've got the contacts," he grumbled. "And I'm not stupid."

"I don't know." I shook my head. "Calling in Security for a reward was dumb."

"Not going to argue I didn't make a mistake. I thought you were kids. I thought there was no way you could get away so I might as well earn some brownie points with Security. I underestimated you." He lowered his voice. "Don't make the same mistake about me."

"You threatening me?" I didn't have fake vampire canines but I still showed him my teeth. "That *really* isn't wise."

He shook his head but didn't look intimidated. Which was fine. We couldn't use him if he was a coward. "If you can get us all to Hephaestus, I've got contacts with a ship refurbishing business there. They can retag your prizes or rebuild them as new ships— the value is in the engines, not the superstructure. I should be able to clear you five percent of the value."

"You're such a kidder, Watton. We'll take 80% of the sales price net of any costs of reconstruction and retagging. How you divide the rest with your buddies is up to you."

"Sixty percent."

"Seventy-five."

"Seventy."

"Done."

He started to reach out a hand, then pulled it back. Nobody wants to shake with a vampire. "The trick," he said, "is getting to Hephaestus. Security knows you're on station."

"They'll be watching for you," I said. "As far as they're concerned, we're a couple of sailors on leave."

"You want to stay or come with us?" I asked the bartender. "You can claim we captured you. Security will probably let you go eventually."

"They'll compost me," he said. "I'll stick with Watton if that's okay with you."

"Like I said, he is going to need help."

"So, give us back our implants," Watton said. "We're all in this together, right?"

"Slaves," I said, "don't get to keep their implants. And guess what, the two of you are slaves we picked up."

"No offense," the bartender said, "but nobody would pay much for a couple of big, fat old guys."

"Yeah, that's a point. Turns out we must be really dumb slaver crewmen."

"How are we getting out?" Ronin asked. "Thanks to your new partner, turncoat-Watton, Security knows we're on planet. They'll be watching and if they see our launch, they'll attack it."

"You're forgetting," I said, "that we've got our slaver friends to help out."

Which is how we did it.

Leaving Gardenia was only a little tricky. I ended up giving Watton and his bartender the spacer IDs and had Nara, me and Ronin play innocent gonna-be-slaves. Watton had to fork over some bribes to the local Security, but that was normal and nobody was suspicious.

The sailors we'd epoxied to the wall were still alive and still stuck where we'd left them.

We chemically removed the epoxy and dragged the sailors with us back to their shuttle.

Which was sealed, of course.

I studied the shuttle's hatch. This was Gardenia. No matter how drunk they were and no matter how big a hurry they'd been to get to the sin-pits of the port, nobody was going to leave their shuttle unlocked.

"I could hack it," Ronin said. "Maybe. But it would take—"

It would take too long but, more importantly, it would warn any of the sailors inside who'd already spent their money and returned to the shuttle.

"Yeah, no," I said. Instead, I grabbed the sailor who looked oldest and shoved his eyeball up to the retinal scanner.

"Open your eye," I said, "or I'll cut it out and use it that way."

"Won't work," he said. "The iris has to be able to respond to light."

"Really? I'd like to see that." I took my knife out and inched it toward his eye.

"Hell." He shoved his face toward the retinal scanner and the airlock portal opened.

"Nice," I said.

As I'd suspected, a couple of sailors were waiting inside but they were drunk, drugged, and exhausted from overindulging in the sin pits of Mjolnir.

Two minutes after I'd jacked the outer hatch, we'd glued both our former captives and their drunk companions into a cargo hold.

"Shuttle Ashir requesting takeoff permission," I lasered the control tower.

"Shuttle Ashir, that's a negative. All traffic is temporarily banned."

"No can do, mission control. We've got drugs on board that require specific climate control."

"Sorry. All traffic is banned."

"We're going to register a complaint with our ship and with port management," I said. "This is completely unacceptable. We have a lot of options other than Gardenia and let me tell you, most of them are a lot more pleasant to visit than this dump."

"We're very sorry. We have a Security emergency."

"Your emergency is not my problem. Taking off in five, four, three, two, one ... I hit the launch button.

"They'll shoot us for sure," Ronin said. "You think they care about killing us?"

"They'd love to kill you and me," I said. "I'm not sure they'd be as keen on killing a group of sailors. If word got out, Mjolnir's trade would take a big hit. What I said about Gardenia having competition is true."

The six Security ships that had tried to trap the *Blood Star* were in orbit, but Mjolnir was a big planetoid and it would take time for them to react.

I wasn't sure we could get away, but I was absolutely sure we wouldn't have a chance if we waited.

So, I got on the horn to Ashir, the shuttle's mother ship, and claimed local Security was trying to steal our harvest of slaves.

They fired a couple of warning shots in the direction of Gardenia's dome, which made Security back off.

I thought we'd won.

Chapter Eighteen

Of course, we couldn't actually dock with Ashir.

Ignoring angry questions from our supposed mother ship, I set down the laser communicator, then fired up all the shuttle's engines to max, heading directly toward Asgard, the nearby star. There wasn't anything in that direction but I hoped Security would lose us in the sun's flare and look for us elsewhere ... or just decide a couple of sailors had gone for a joy-ride and forget about us.

Hopes are meant to be shattered, and it wasn't long before I saw the glowing streaks that indicated other ships had joined the hunt.

"All ships, Security offers free docking for a year to any ship that captures or destroys the shuttle hijacked from Ashir."

I recognized Harding's voice. Damn, that man had a thing for me.

"They connected your raid on my place with the shuttle," Watton guessed.

"Thanks to you calling Security in." Ronin put a snarl in his voice.

"If you'd seen the reward, you would have—"

"Bull. I don't sell out my friends ... or my business partners."

"Thanks for the teamwork, you guys," I said. "I don't think I could manage this without your nagging each other." I was pretty sure they could hear the sarcasm but if they missed it, I wouldn't mind rubbing their noses in it. What is it about men that makes them want to play the blame game?

"How about we drop off a sailor every few thousand kiilometers," Nara suggested. "When they slow to pick them up, we could get away."

"You think they'd stop?" Ronin shook his head.

"I've got my doubts," I admitted. But it did give me an idea.

"Well..." We hadn't heard from the bartender lately, so I figured he was about entitled to his chance to talk. "So, what are we going to do?"

I checked my rebreather, then picked up the whisker-laser microphone.

"This is Captain Lorne calling captains of pursuing ships."

"Kari, this is your last chance to surrender. Save your sister, at least."

I was pretty sure this was at least the fifth or sixth 'last' chance Harding had given me.

"We've taken a dozen sailors hostage," I told Harding. "We'll drop them off, one by one. We're giving them enough air for an hour in the vacuum but any longer than that, you've got dead sailors on your conscience. And you've got some ugly public relations with any merchant who thinks about spacing with you."

"You hurt any of the hostages," Harding said, "I'll make sure you hurt even more."

Like he didn't plan on hurting me no matter what I did. I didn't think it would do Mjolnir's business much good if they lost a bunch of visiting sailors. I also didn't think Harding was thinking rationally enough to stop and pick them up.

"Toss the first sailor," I ordered. Then I switched off the microphone.

"That would be murder," Nara protested. "You just said they weren't going to stop."

"Yeah. I thought I'd double-check on that, though. Just to be absolutely sure."

Ronin shrugged. "I guess it can't hurt. Us, anyway."

I peered into the video feed from the cargo hold where we'd glued our sailors. They were slime. They'd tried to enslave me. And I was pretty sure any one of them would have dumped me, another sailor or even their mother into space if they thought it might buy them another few hours of life.

"Which one we going to toss first?" Nara asked.

"Yeah, sure, easy choice. Let's rig up one of the suits."

I set the suit's AI to synthesize the voice of one of the sailors, added eighty kilos of biomass from the kitchenette, and then we dumped it out the airlock.

Harding could have deputized one of the slower Security fighters to pick up the hostage without really impacting his fighting strength. Or he could have paid one of the trailing merchant ships and shuttles to do the job. But he didn't and nobody decelerated when they passed the floating and signaling suit.

"Maybe they knew it was a dummy," Ronin suggested.

"Yeah. And maybe Harding is so desperate to catch us, he'll do anything."

I tight-beamed Shena, back on the launch, and told her to get ready to meet up with us... somehow.

Then I reset the auto-pilot to drive the shuttle at maximum acceleration for two hours, after which it would heave to and send out distress signals. That taken care of, I checked the air charges in our rebreathers and snipped the radios off Watten's and the bartender's, whose name turned out to be Persi, suits. Finally I led Ronin, Nara, Watten and Persi to the airlock, cycled us through, and stepped into space.

From Mjolnir, Thor was a monster. In space, it was even bigger. Whenever I looked at it, I felt as if we were being sucked into the gravity well instead of safely in orbit about it. Then again, maybe we would. Although Gardenia was in orbit, we'd accelerated a lot after our abrupt departure. We'd broken that orbit but I wasn't sure if we'd achieved a stable new orbit around the gas giant.

One by one, the chasing ships flashed by us, ignoring our suits and the distress signals they were sending. Security's ship engines annihilating matter-anti-matter a bit faster than was safe as they tried to climb to the point where they could use their jump drives.

Our little launch, which had tagged onto the back of the fleet, along with the shuttle's mother-ship and a few other armed merchants, picked us up about twenty minutes later.

"You guys all right?" Shena demanded as we stripped our rebreathers.

"We'll probably have some radiation sickness," I admitted. "And I'm going to need blood soon. But so far we're alive which is better than—"

My words were cut off by a flash of light on the screen.

"Looks like they blew up the shuttle," Cassie said.

"No way," I protested. "It would have been sending its surrender messages by now. How could they—"

"You're a vampire," Nara reminded me. "And we're vampire friends. Capturing you just means more trouble—and more chances for something to go wrong. Plus, they might actually have to pay a reward if someone else caught you. Blowing you out of space avoids those complications. And they can blame the dead sailors on you rather than admit they sailed by them."

I nodded slowly. I didn't want to think that way but Nara was right—Security wasn't behaving rationally. Which meant, I was acting crazy when I kept thinking they would.

It also meant I'd been responsible for the deaths of the sailors I'd left locked in the shuttle's cargo hold. I should have tossed them out with us.

I took a minute to contemplate that. I wanted longer. Wanted to wallow in the realization that every decision I made seemed to cost someone their life. But I didn't have time to fall apart. The sailors were gone but my crew wasn't. And if I didn't get back to them with a place where we could re-supply, they were going to die as well.

"So," I said to Watton, "in addition to transuranics, antimatter and water, we need a place to unload ex-slavers. A place where they won't just be recycled into new slavers because we intend to put an end to that entire business."

"You do that, who are you going to pirate on?"

"You know," I said, "that's a problem I'm looking forward to having. I suspect I'll die of old age before we make more than a dent in the trade. The galaxy isn't close to running out of rich disgusting old men who like hurting children. Now, are your business partners going to help us, or should we just space you and let Security pick you up?"

"You wouldn't—"

Maybe he was right. I'd just sent eight sailors to their death and felt terrible but I was also sick of Watton's attitude. "Don't tell me what I would and wouldn't do, Watton. Because I'll do whatever I have to to keep my friends alive. Guess what … so far, you're not helping and you're certainly not acting like you want to be one of those friends"

We'd tried to be stealthy after Shena had picked us up, limping away from the chase like we'd blown an engine. Maybe that bought us some time but about ten minutes after they blew up the shuttle the armada flipped around and accelerated after us.

"They must have run us in their Identify Friend-Foe database," Shena said.

"Full speed," I ordered. "We going to make it?"

Shena wrinkled her nose and jammed the throttle full ahead. "Calculating." A couple minutes later she shook her head. "Going to be close but I don't think so."

The launch's anti-grav units whining as they kept us from getting smashed flat under full acceleration.

We huddled around the holo-plot and watched.

For a long time, it seemed that Shena's concerns were overblown. The distance between our shuttle and the chasing ships continued to grow as they struggled to shed delta-v and we accelerated.

After about fifteen minutes, three of the ships were gaining on us quickly while the remainder of the chase fleet scattered, apparently giving up the chase.

"Those gotta be Security's frigates," bartender-Persi offered. "Spent a lot of money on them. Supposed to be fast."

Yeah, they were fast. Way too fast. I'd been sure we'd be able to use that speed against them when they chased after the shuttle but they were racking up deceleration way faster than we could.

"I don't think we can pull the jumping into space thing again," Shena said. "They'll have figured out how we got away and be sure to check on any bodies we launch. Of course, we don't have anyone else to pick us up, either."

Ronin nodded excitedly. "But if we load the suits with explosives, when they check, boom."

I was no space lawyer but I was pretty sure anyone who rigged up booby traps on supposed bodies broadcasting S.O.S. messages would be hunted by everyone... sort of like a vampire. While I might be universally despised, my girls didn't have to be.

"I'm betting," I said, "that they won't check, they'll burn anything that looks like it might be us."

Everyone agreed with that which didn't make me feel good. Why couldn't someone have pointed out some obvious flaw in the logic which would mean we could get away?

I realized, though, that everyone was looking at me. Like I was supposed to supply the next miracle.

"How long until translation velocity?" I asked Shena.

"Twenty-seven minutes on my mark... mark."

"How long until we're Security has us in missile range?"

"Twenty minutes until extreme range," Ronin said. "Twenty-three until they're close enough to pretty much guarantee a hit."

"So we need to create four minutes."

"Creating time would be a good trick," Ronin said. "You've managed some good ones up until now but that would top them all."

I think I turned a little red. Where had that come from? Ronin was supposed to be snarky and sarcastic.

"Suppose we try dropping missiles inside skinsuits," I said.

"You know," Ronin said, "someone was just saying what a bad idea that is."

"No S.O.S. Just the skinsuits. Then we program the missiles' target acquisition system to follow a lethal-grade laser strike back to the source. If it just gets painted by radar or something, or if it's picked up, it does nothing."

It was a crazy plan. Our launch didn't have many missiles but it had enough to put up at least some defense. By tossing them out, we'd be essentially letting Corporate Security destroy them without even turning on their countermeasures.

Ronin gave me a strange look. "This isn't some sort of vampire plot to get us all killed so you can suck our blood is it?"

I shrugged. His words stung me even though I knew they shouldn't. "Anyone have a better idea?"

****

Antiship missiles are about the size of a human wearing a heavy suit including oxygen tanks. And their nuclear fuel gives them a heat signature. We spent a couple of minutes reprogramming the missile A.I.s so they'd lock only onto an anti-personnel laser strike and a few more making sure that the hardsuits we were dumping didn't automatically go into S.O.S. broadcast mode.

Then we shoved the missiles out an airlock, then went back to watch the screens.

The missiles continued with the same momentum they'd had when we dumped them, but we were still accelerating so we left them behind. Although they were moving in the same direction as the chasing ships, because those ships had achieved an acceleration even greater than our own, the missiles would appear to be accelerating in their direction.

"Maybe they won't even notice them and they'll smash into some of the missiles," Nara said. "That would slow them down."

Ronin shook his head. "Space is too big, you know that. Kari's plan is the only one that gives us a chance."

I wasn't sure why his support felt so good.

Which was about the only thing that felt good. I realized I wasn't shaking from the suspense, I needed blood.

I'd accepted blood from everyone on my team on the launch but that was when they'd offered. Now, a part of me wanted to grab on and sink my teeth into all of them, to suck not just the little bit of blood they offered and that kept me alive, but enough to fill me.

I looked at Ronin, then at Nara. Ronin was bigger, but Nara was the tougher opponent. I'd have to catch her by surprise, take her out quickly, then turn on Ronin, Shena and the others. I could—"

I was way further down that mental path than I should have gotten when I realized where I was headed. Maybe Security was right to hate vampires.

I just needed to ask and one of them would offer me one of those little thimbles-full of blood. That would keep me going... until the next time.

I took a deep breath. I'd promised my mother I would take care of Shena and now I was her biggest danger. Maybe I should have jumped out with the missiles.

I forced my eyes away from my crewmates and to the monitors. I could wait a little longer. Couldn't I?

Our acceleration had left the missiles far behind and now the Security destroyers were approaching them.

The missiles and destroyers converged on the screen and nothing happened.

Nara reset the monitor resolution and the missiles were still hundreds of kilometers away but converging very quickly.

"Doesn't look like they're taking the bait," Shena said. "They're not picking them up but they're not—"

At a million kilometers an hour, a few hundred kilometers can be crossed very quickly.

My vision blurred. I needed blood so bad.

"They're launching." Ronin pounded my arm in excitement. "Security must have hit them with antipersonnel just like you knew they would."

"Must have," I murmured.

"Scrambling. They're launching all sorts of countermeasures," Nara said.

No surprise. They were military ships. Of course they'd have antimissile defenses. But those defenses were designed to take out attacks at far greater distances.

"They got one," Shena said. "Oops. Another."

"But one got through." Ronin's voice broke in his excitement. "The lead destroyer has lost acceleration."

"The others are still coming, though," Nara said.

I looked at the screen but it all went blurry. Then everything went black.

****

"You are a complete idiot." Shena's voice sounded a million miles away.

I couldn't see so I tried to grab whatever was covering my eyes, only to realize they were tied down.

"What happened?" My voice sounded like something ground out by a malware bot.

"You went nuts just as we got away from Security, that's what happened." It was Ronin's voice this time.

"Well I'm not nuts any more. So untie me and let me get to work."

"Oh no." It was Shena again. "Ronin and I have been talking this over. You need to agree not to do this again."

Ronin and her. Why did that grate wrong with me? I should be happy for my sister, right?

I pulled my brain back to what she'd said. "Do what?"

"You know what." Shena sounded mad. "You tried to tough it out, didn't you? Decided you were too good to ask for blood. Maybe you even thought you'd die some sort of silly sacrifice to keep us all safe. Well, we're safer with you alive and healthy. Nobody wants a noble sacrifice. None of us have any use for a corpse, even a vampire corpse. And if you ever thought you were keeping your promise to mother, you can forget it. Every time you do this, you're making me less safe."

That was a low blow. She had to know I felt bad about letting down mother. "I think—"

"Look, just promise you'll ask when you need blood or we're keeping you tied down."

"Like I'll be a big help to you that way."

"Like you were a big help just now. Look at Ronin."

"My eyes are covered. I can't—"

The ripping sound was accompanied by the sensation of half my hair and all of my eyebrows being ripped out. And white ship-light glared into my eyes like a laser.

I blinked and Shena swam into focus. She had a black eye and bruises along her left arm. Ronin was hanging behind her but I could see enough to make out that he had a cast on one leg and a fresh scar that ran from his scalp line down to his chin, barely missing an eye. A bandage covered one cheek.

"What happened to you?" I demanded. "Did Watton and—"

"You want to know what happened?" Shena shouted. "You did. You waited too long to get blood and your instincts took over. Now, will you please promise to ask when you need blood? We need you to help us but not if we have to spend all our time worrying that you're going to freak out again. It was scary."

I looked at the two of them again. I'd assumed I would sort of fade away. But my vampire side hadn't been on the same page. I hated that I couldn't control myself, but at least now I knew.

Either I needed to keep drinking blood forever or I needed to turn myself over to Security. I trusted they could find a final solution.

"Kari," Ronin said, "I know you feel guilty about what they made you. I know a part of you wants to run away. But we're your friends so you have to trust us. We want you to stay. Not just because we have a better chance at survival with you, but because we like you."

He brushed a knuckle against my arm. His muscles were tight from fear that I'd turn on him again, but he still did it."

"All right." I sighed, then realized I'd still been looking for ways to run away from my sister, my promise to my mother, and my friends.

Running was over. Both for me and for my pirate band.

****

Take most people away from their homes, their friends, their assets, and they've got trouble. I'd worried that Watton would be in the same boat, but my concerns were unwarranted. Between the assets he'd secreted around the galaxy and what seemed to be a trans-planetary network of criminals, he settled into his new home on Hephaestus, a run-down orbital platform in even worse shape than Gardenia, and started sending a steady stream of transuranics, design enhancements, water and carbon, and especially news about slave ship schedules.

Over the next six months, we raided eight more slave ships, freeing close to a thousand slaves (about fifty boys, the rest girls), and avoiding Security's attempts to counter us.

Following our original plan, we sold most of the ships we'd captured, although we kept a number of fast launches to let us move quickly to board enemy slave-ships and evacuate the slaves in the one case where a captain decided to be a hero and sabotaged his own ship. We'd let that captain stay on his ship.

Some of the freed slaves actually had places to return, and a few were able to take others with them. Some were happy to settle on a nice planet we'd found, or work in the orbital shipyard we set up. Still, our crew swelled to the point where I was able to equip a second ship for our fleet.

After a month of refitting our new pirate ship, we returned to Hephaestus to pick up the latest slaver schedules and plans.

Watton looked grim as he crossed the airlock from his shuttle.

"What do you have for me?" I demanded.

"I, uh, that is ... I've been working hard."

I didn't trust him, but I didn't think he'd sell us out. First, he was in too deep and betraying us would give him a reputation he'd never shake with the other criminals, and second, he was making too much money factoring our prizes.

"Working hard on what?"

"That's the thing." If anything, he'd gained weight in the months since we'd left Gardenia. His face was a slick mask of sweat and he really needed to get his health nanobes looked at because he was losing the battle to whatever microbes make sweat stink.

"I'll bite," I said. "What thing?"

He flinched a little at the word "bite" which didn't bother me at all. I wanted him to be more afraid of me than he was of Security.

"They've gone convoy," he said. "No slave ships are sailing without at least a couple of destroyer-class escort ships."

"Where are they getting all the escort ships?"

"A lot of rich men depend on slave girls. And everyone is afraid of vampires."

"Tell me something I don't know, Watton."

"So, all those planets and platforms and businesses are lending Security their gunships. They have hundreds. They've embargoed planets and platforms that won't support them and they've swept up a few of the slaves you already freed so they know everything about us that the slaves know."

I nodded. We didn't tell the girls we rescued everything because we knew re-capture was a possibility. Still, I hated the idea of anyone back in Security's hands, especially since we knew Harding liked to torture girls.

We'd known that Security would react… they had to with the losses we caused them. Unfortunately, they'd reacted more completely than I would have guessed possible. Each corporation and planet guarded its fleets jealously. I had calculated at most a few of them would actually turn their precious ships over to Security. The threat to their supply of little girls, coupled with their fear of vampires, had proved a more potent force than I'd anticipated.

"You could go after merchant ships," Watton said. "So far, they've only been convoying the slavers. The worst part is, the engineers at Hephaestus weren't as careful as they should have been, so some of the planets who bought your ships got caught… and Security is attacking them. They've got Njold under siege right now. Which means, every single customer I had lined up is backing off. Nobody wants Security attacking them."

That was bad news. The biggest problem pirates face wasn't enemy ships tasked with hunting them down—space is huge and it just wasn't that difficult to hide. The problem is finding supply and markets for pillage. Without friendly ports, eventually we'd run out of transuranics for our missiles, antimatter for our engines and deuterium to fuel our fusion generators—and we'd be defenseless when Security finally tracked us down. If we didn't starve first.

"We've got to break that siege," Ronin said. "Njold stuck their necks out for us. We can't let them fall to Security. When we help them, that'll encourage new customers and make Security look weak."

If they'd stuck their necks out, it was because they'd never thought they'd get caught and we sold them ships at ridiculous prices. Certainly if anything had happened to us, they would have moved on without a backward glance.

That didn't matter now, though. Ronin was right. If we let Security roll over Njold, nobody would do business with us for fear they'd be next. But we weren't strong enough even to take on a convoy. What made us think we could break a siege?

"You have a list of the ships besieging their ports?" I asked.

Watton nodded, his forehead gleaming with sweat. "Of course. For the small price of only—"

"Can it, Watton. I'm not going to pay for the privilege of pulling your trading partners out of the fire."

He looked like he wanted to argue, went so far as to open his mouth a couple of times. Finally, though, he shrugged. "Two destroyers, one cruiser, a couple of frigates and a makeshift carrier for each."

"Tell me about the carriers."

"Nothing special. Old merchant ships with a bunch of the cargo holds converted to support fighters. Probably only about thirty fighters per ship and the fighters have no jump capability, but in normal-space, those little one-seaters can pack a punch and if Security loses a few, it's no big deal."

"Earth was big on carriers," Nara said.

Watton shrugged. "Earth's carriers were bigger, faster, tougher, and carried hundreds of fighters rather than just a couple of dozen. But Earth couldn't afford to lose any. Since they're just using old merchants as carriers, Security doesn't mind if you shoot up the whole lot of them ... as long as they take you out in the process."

"Well," I said, "we couldn't handle a couple of destroyers. Add a cruiser and we're hopelessly outclassed even without the carriers and fighters."

"So we're running?" Ronin made it sound like that was the worst thing we could do.

"I don't mind fighting if I have a chance at winning. But I'm not going to start a fight we couldn't—"

"You already started the fight," Ronin said. "You started it when you went after your sister. We couldn't possibly win but you didn't give up ... not then."

"I get it, Ronin." I got it, but I still wasn't interested in some *yolo* attack.

I'd hoped I'd never have to use them, but when we got back to the Blood Star, I gave Shena, who had the controls, the coordinates I'd held in reserve. Whatever Ronin thought, I wasn't about to give up. But I hadn't saved all these girls just to throw away their lives.

Chapter Nineteen

We caught a slave ship that hadn't gotten the word about convoys. After adding it to our fleet, we were three ships entering the vast no-man's land that surrounded ancient Earth.

I ordered double-watches and camped near the signaling station so I'd be ready when we ran into trouble… and we were going to run into trouble.

Two days after crossing the invisible boundary between far-space and Earth-space, we made contact.

"Unidentified ship," the whiny Earth accent was unmistakable. "Heave-to for boarding."

"This is the independent slave-fighter *Blood Star*," I shot back. I'd decided that 'slave fighter' sounded better than 'pirate.' "The Security Corporation from the further stars is besieging planetary systems that are aiding in our efforts to combat human slavery. We're calling on Earth's fleets to assist us in the defeat of this insidious disease."

There was a half-hour delay before the response came.

"*Blood Star*, this is Captain Wendy Bogain of *E.F. New South Wales*. You will cease acceleration at this point. I will convey your message to Admiral Noomis for consideration. Do not make any attempt to withdraw from space under the control of Earth-Fleet or you will be destroyed."

****

Earth-Fleet was worse off than I'd imagined.

I didn't see a single sailor who looked like he could stand up to a punch, let alone fight back. Their ships were in bad repair, and none of them was younger than the *Blood Star*.

Admiral Noomis, along with her flag captain and Captain Bogain, met me in her Secondary Battle Unit—possibly because he was worried I carried some hidden explosive but more likely, I thought, because he didn't want me to see how depleted her bridge crew and bridge equipment was.

I laid out our position—that we were fighting the slave trade and that Earth had historically stood against slavery.

"While it's true," Noomis said, "that Earth-Fleet is technically at war with any slave trade, we haven't ventured outside of Earth-space for over fifty years. If you know your history, we won every battle we fought, but Earth never had the resources to replace our losses. The corporations who rule the out-stars seem able to churn out new ships with reckless abandon."

"Not quite," I said. "Ships are still expensive. But you're right, the outer stars do have ship construction sites. They've also got transuranics for missiles and matter-antimatter engines and…" I shifted my glance from the admiral to her crewmen… "And food."

"Be that as it may," Noomis said, "I don't understand what you want from us. If you wish to join Earth-Fleet, we could—"

I shook my head. I appreciated that she hadn't mentioned reclaiming the Blood Star, one of my big worries, but looking at this group of starving sailors didn't make me want to sign up. "You've already made it clear that Earth-Fleet is a dying institution, Admiral. I have a lot of respect for what you've done over the decades, but Earth can't afford the fleet, which is why you're scavenging and stealing."

Noomis looked like she wanted to object. She managed just to shake her head. "As I said," she said, "I fail to understand what you're looking for."

"Earth-Fleet is in trouble," I said, "because it relies on Earth for support and Earth has no support to offer it. If you had planets and platforms of your own, you could—"

"I'm afraid Earth outlasted its welcome in the outer system when it overran spacer systems," Noomis said. "As far as near-Earth systems, we're already using—"

"I'm not talking about milking systems to feed Earth," I said. "Earth could have cut back on its population but chose to expand it instead. They've got more people than they can feed now and they'll continue to expand if we did manage to feed what they've got. Frankly, from what I've heard, I don't think the rest of the galaxy's human population could make much difference even if they all worked at nothing but feeding Earth."

"So—" Noomis started.

I cut her off again. Interrupting was a bad habit but I seemed stuck with it. "But from what I've seen, what's left of Fleet isn't that big. One decent agricultural planet could feed Fleet."

Noomis looked like she'd been kicked in the gut. "You're saying we should betray Earth?"

I shook my head. "I'm saying that you're now a burden on Earth ... a burden they can't afford. If you could be self-sustaining, Earth would be better off and you'd be better off. Not that Earth won't suffer from its overpopulation, but how are you helping them now?"

She narrowed her eyes. "Somehow, I don't think you've come to us because your heart was filled with compassion for Earth's suffering or for Earth-Fleet's troubles. Give it to me straight. What do you want from us and what do we get in return?"

I grinned. "Now you're talking. Have you ever heard of Plautus? It's an agricultural world orbiting ...."

Chapter Twenty

I'd figured that, if I could get Earth-Fleet involved, we'd head straight to Njold and break the siege. Noomis persuaded me to take an indirect approach. Earth-fleet and our little pirate squadron translated into orbit around Thor. Within hours, Fleet's fighters were buzzing Gardenia, shooting up orbital defenses, and generally making nuisances of themselves.

Less than a day after we'd arrived, ground-based Security executives shuttled to Noomis's flagship with their tails between their legs.

Because I'd lived there, I wasn't surprised that their first offer was, basically, to sell out Plautus and keep Mjolnir. After all, Plautus was a bunch of religious farmers. Whatever they paid Security for protection wouldn't cover the costs of an actual battle, even assuming Security could win.

If I hadn't been there, Noomis would probably have taken the deal... and added to the enmity Earth-Fleet had earned over the decades. Disguised in an Earth-Fleet uniform ... which was tight on me even though I was still a skinny, small-for-my-age teen, I kept an encrypted com link to the admiral and added to her demands. Fleet was hungry, and not in a good way. But access to an agricultural world wasn't the answer they needed and it certainly wasn't the answer I needed for my rescued ex-slaves. I needed a station—someplace where we could trade, repair our fleets, even pick over the old mine tailings for transuranics the first mining ventures had missed. If we were going to war against Security's slave trade, we needed the whole Asgard system.

Security moaned and whined about Noomis's demands. They also shipped out on a barely air-tight merchant ship. Within six hours of their departure, Fleet marines hit the ground. From what I learned later, they ignored the women, alcohol and drugs and headed directly for anyplace with food.

The fighters turned their attention to Plauton. That, after all, was where the real food opportunities could be found.

Ronin and I landed in Gardenia about six hours behind the marines.

Mjolnir station had been going downhill for at least fifty years and Security had stripped what was left of everything they could. Its inhabitants were mostly Hasro addicts. But while its drydocks were mothballed, and half its orbital solar panels were misaligned and out of service, those were all problems that could be fixed with determination and manpower. Between Earth-Fleet and the unemployed drug addicts of Gardenia, the manpower was available. And I had just the man for the job—Watton was a slimebag, but he knew how to motivate druggies.

Without the questionable protection Security offered them, Plautus capitulated almost instantly to Earth-Fleet's demands. Which, basically, were that it implement modern agricultural technologies and increase its agricultural surplus while doing away with its practice of selling surplus girls into slavery.

Run properly, Plautus wouldn't make much of a dent in Earth's hunger ... but it could easily feed Earth-Fleet even without making any improvements. With the changes Fleet demanded, it could generate a surplus that would pay for Earth's latest solar technologies, advanced robotic systems and medical advances—which would let its population live in style. Since according to their religious beliefs, living in style was a sign of divine favor, negotiations weren't too challenging.

Noomis still looked like a walking skeleton when she called me to her bridge two weeks after we'd invaded the Asgard system. Skinny or not, I suspected the smile on her face was the first she'd had since becoming admiral a couple of decades earlier.

"Your man Watton is an unscrupulous degenerate who's skimming two percent of everything we spend on repairs and rebuilding."

"Really," I said. "I told him he could have up to three. You might have your bean-counters double-check."

She nodded. "Still, a good choice. Repairs are going well."

"But…" If everything was going so well, why weren't we relieving the siege?

"I thought," she said, "that you'd want to know that elements of Security fleet probed Asgard's Oort cloud. Over the past twenty-four hours, our destroyers and carriers saw them off."

"And?"

"You know I've been concerned that the corporations will unite against Fleet, especially after we signed a truce with Security. Their illegal attack gives us a *casus belli* that could give corporations who don't like Security a reason to hold back."

"Lucky for you that this happened, huh?"

She shrugged. "Perhaps their spies gave them the wrong idea of our preparedness. It turns out, your friend Watton has some useful connections."

"He's not exactly a friend. But he does have a vampire fetish."

"Yeah, I got that."

"So, we're finally going after Njold."

"That was our agreement."

"Earth-Fleet has a reputation of changing agreements when convenient. I'd prefer a more definitive answer."

"Ah, yes." Noomis had the grace to look a little ashamed of herself. "There is one little matter. We need food and Njold can produce a surplus. You can't expect us to fight your battles for free."

I sighed. "System Njold provided support for the anti-slavery movement. They're under siege by Security. If we treat them like a prize, the other systems will all unite against us. It's only because Security overreached, and because, frankly, of the information we've been able to spread about their dependence on slave trading, that you've been able to secure your control over the Asgard system."

"There is a water-bearing planet, Bergthora, in the Njold system," Noomis said as if she hadn't heard a word I'd said. "It could support a significant human population."

"For what?" I demanded. "You could move a billion people from Earth there and nobody on Earth would notice the difference."

Noomis shrugged. "True. But Fleet's ships are poor places to raise children. With our own world, families could take a year or decade to farm, raise children, recharge, then return to Fleet. Our agreement with Plautus gives us food but we need a place of our own."

"You're Earth-Fleet. What's wrong with Earth as your place."

"You're joking, of course."

I hadn't been, but she was right—Earth was already crammed full. "This water-bearing planet is unoccupied?"

"There are miners but that's about it."

"What about them?"

"They can continue working under our administration or we'll ship them elsewhere."

"To a system of their choice?"

Noomis smiled. "Your squadron has more access to the outer stars than does Fleet."

"All right," I said. "We'll position settlement as a trade benefit for Njold. If necessary, I'll transport them on my ships. Anything else stopping us from moving forward?"

Noomis shook her head. "I do want you to understand that Fleet intends to stop after this. We need refitting, need to tend to our new homes. Once the siege of Njold is broken, we'll attempt to negotiate a permanent peace with Security."

"What about the slave trade. You—"

"There will always be evils that need fighting. We'll contain any trade between Earth sector, Asgard System and Njold. Beyond that…" she shrugged. "We aren't going to try to police all of humanity."

She sounded definite, but I didn't want to fight Security single-handed. Which is why I'd brought in Fleet in the first place. "So, you get what you need and abandon us?"

"You're free to trade with any systems under our control. From my reading of history, this is a huge advantage for any pirate. Even if I wanted to do more, I'm limited. It's been fifty years since the last time any of our ships drydocked. We're low on missiles, low on fusion mass, low on food, low on blood, low on—"

"Low on blood?" I gasped out the word before I could think.

"Ah. Perhaps I shouldn't have said anything about—"

"But you did. What about blood?"

"Nobody knows why, but a number of our sailors have developed immune deficiencies which can be dealt with only

185

through ingesting whole blood. We aren't just starving, many of us have a peculiar disease that—"

"You've got vampires?"

"We don't use that word."

Yeah? Well, not using a word didn't mean a whole lot to me. "You know where the vampires come from, don't you?"

"I assume it's some sort of—"

"Don't assume anything. Security has a poison they use to take out adults while sparing children, who are then taken as slaves. If you're in the middle, you become a vampire. Considering what Security thinks of Earth-Fleet, it isn't a huge surprise that they'd use it on you."

Noomis nodded. "I suppose it's possible."

"So," I gave her my best grin. "Now that you know, don't you think we should work together to wipe them out?"

She shook her head. "No."

****

Earth-Fleet had been locked within the overpopulated Earth sector for so long, Security had never imagined they'd come out... especially for something as trivial as to interfere in the slave trade. So we'd approached Asgard sector without being spotted and with the bulk of Security's fleets doing convoy duty and besieging Njold.

That was then. Unfortunately, they'd used the time Fleet had needed to consolidate their control over Asgard system to prepare for a fight and they'd guessed we'd be coming for Njold.

Noomis had brought most of her portion of Earth-Fleet from Earth sector to Asgard system. After all, Earth sector didn't have anything worth attacking and its orbital fortresses could deal with anything Security threw at it. Now, though, Noomis had Mjolnir and Plautus to defend. If she went all-out in releaving Njold, Security would hit Asgard. So, she left most of Earth-Fleet orbiting Thor. Between guarding Mjolnir Station, building orbital fortresses, negotiating for Hasro-free blood supplies and continued repairs and upgrades, she couldn't spare more than a couple of squadrons—plus our pirates.

If we'd had a couple more months, she could have put most of Fleet's powerful warships into operation, but a handful of dispatch torpedos had reached us from Njold. If they didn't get help soon, they would have to surrender. We just didn't have the time.

Noomis promised to follow with what she could when she could, but sent me and my pirate squadron out first as a vanguard and scout.

We translated into Njold's Kuiper belt well off the eliptic where I'd calculated we would be harder to spot and got the bad news.

Security had taken the time we'd given them to construct a double-sphere of orbital fortresses—the inner one facing Njold's defenses and the outer one facing out. Ships on Njold couldn't translate out because they were too near the star's gravity well. Unfortunately, that wasn't true of Security. So, no blockade was possible—they could translate directly from inside the ring.

They might have dozens more ships lying silent but thirty ships and at least a hundred orbital fortresses were active.

"Looks like we're too late."Nara said.

"We don't really need Njold," Shena said. "We can always trade with Fleet in Gardenia."

"And leave people who took a chance on us to die?" Ronin argued. "We can't do that."

"Exactly how does it help them if we smear ourselves thin on Security's fortresses?" Shena demanded. "Besides, they only helped us because they thought they could get rich doing it, not because they cared about the girls."

"We don't have to take them alone," I reminded my crew. "Fleet will be here soon."

"A little bit of a worn-out Fleet," Shena said.

"They're what we've got. And we are going to help Njold."

"I'm all for that," Ronin said. "I suppose you have a plan."

"Yeah, about that."

A plan would be great. While I waited for one to hit me, I took the *Blood Star* on a bunch of short translations. Security knew we were coming, so I figured we'd keep them awake and feel out their defenses.

Orbital forts are great for defense. They're powerful and have massive anti-missile complexes. A triple of forts, and they're always deployed in threes, supported each other, and could chew up an entire fleet if one was dumb enough to attack them.

They're not especially fast but they're not purely orbital—if they couldn't be navigated at all, they'd be sitting ducks to supermassive weapons like accelerated asteroids. What they can't do is translate—if they could do that, they'd be ships.

So, we approached, threw a few missiles, then translated a few million kilometers away to watch the reaction. At least the defenders on Njold would see we were doing something.

We spent a couple of days of doing that, sending message torpedoes back to Noomis and Fleet and wondering why the heck they hadn't followed as promised. I didn't spot any weaknesses in Security's blockade, but hoped that Noomis might have better luck with her Earth-tech battle A.I.s. Assuming Noomis hadn't decided I was an inconvenience and sent me to die.

Three days after we'd arrived, the ship's alarms all went off together.

I'd somehow fallen asleep at the weapon control center. When I jerked awake, I pushed myself back so quickly I knocked Ronin, who'd also fallen asleep leaning against me, to the ground.

"Huh?"

It wasn't very articulate but I still grabbed the command back from Nara.

The Star's A.I.s highlighted the orbital fort we'd been playing with. At first, I couldn't see anything strange about it. Ronin brought it to my attention.

"It translated. Not far but—"

"Forts don't—"

"So it's a ship in disguise. Whatever you call it, it's coming for us."

"Okay. Let's vector out of here." I tuned into the A.I. and looked for an escape path—I wasn't really worried. A ship that massive would have to be slow.

I calculated and sent the course to the navigation A.I.

"Should we try to slow them down with some missiles?" Ronin had taken over weapons when I'd grabbed navigation.

"Don't waste our firepower," I said. "They'll—"

"Oh, no." Shena didn't say she'd told us so but I heard the meaning in her tone. "Looks like that jerk, Harding, is playing his games again."

"What … oh." Once again, the tactical board lit up as what looked like a hundred Security ships fired their engines. Harding seemed fixated on setting traps. This time he'd caught us.

"Missiles inbound." Nara reported the news about a tenth of a second after the A.I. detected it. It was a pretty fast reaction but I didn't see how that helped.

The A.I. and I plotted vectors and neither of us spotted a way out. We'd let ourselves get too close to what I'd supposed to be semi-stationary forts and now we couldn't manage the acceleration we needed for translation.

"You know, you guys," I said, "I really didn't want it to end this way, but if it has to end, I'm glad we'll go down fighting."

"You giving up?" Ronin looked like I'd just insulted his mother.

"No, I'm not giving up. But I am recognizing the situation. We aren't going to be able to find the weak point like we did last time he trapped us. Unfortunately it looks to me like he learned more from that little expedition than I did."

"Uh," Ronin stood, then stepped over to me. "If we're going to die, could I maybe…"

I had no idea what he was talking about until he bent over and kissed me.

I had to keep myself from biting, which wasn't a good thing. But he tasted good and his racing pulse was distracting. Not so distracting that I couldn't enjoy the kiss—until I remembered my sister. She was the one with the crush. She'd think …

"Don't be silly," Shena told me before I could say anything. "Ronin likes you."

And he'd only told me when he was sure we were all going to die. I wasn't sure I liked that logic.

"Maybe we'd better worry about Security," Nara said.

"Yeah, maybe we'd better." Logically that didn't make sense. If we couldn't get away, shouldn't we just enjoy the few minutes we had to live? But that kind of logic had never done much for me.

"We might have a chance if we head toward Njold," Nara said. "We'd have to avoid the big fortresses but they're not really designed to chase down fast little pirate ships."

It wasn't a bad idea. Being trapped inside the siege wasn't ideal but it was preferable to dying outside.

I figured *we* might make it—but the *Blood Star* wasn't alone and the slower ships in our squadron didn't have a chance. On the other hand, they might make it to freedom if we distracted Harding. Which had to be the right answer in terms of saving lives. There were a lot more ex-slaves on the other three ships in the squadron than there were on the *Star*.

"The rest of the squadron, head for Njold," I said. "We're going to provide cover." *And die*, I didn't add.

Chapter Twenty-One

"Well," I said, "charging full speed at Harding worked last time we tried it. Here we go."

"I don't think it'll work this time," Shena said.

I had a flashback to the time we'd been locked in the cage and those sailors had all come down to take advantage of us. This was a lot like that—bigger, stronger, better-armed attackers and me. Only that time, they hadn't been expecting a fight. This time, they knew what we were capable of. After all, every ship in my small squadron had once belonged to Security.

Knowing the situations weren't parallel didn't stop the flashbacks. Finally, I let myself listen to my intuition. For a few moments, there was nothing but silence inside of me. While all around my crew shouted out commands, the ship shuddered with the release of missiles and anti-missile fire, and Nara passed my orders to the other ships in my squadron.

The sound of Nara's voice, though, brought with it a picture—I flashed back to her slow-motion dance of destruction in the slave-pen.

Okay, if that's where my intuition wanted me to go, I guessed we were in as good a place as any.

I closed my eyes to tune out everything but the images the *Star*'s A.I. sent to my implant and read out navigational changes.

I didn't need to vocalize for the *Star* to respond, but if Ronin and Nara were going to operate the offensive missiles and if Shena was to have a chance with the defensive rail-guns, they had to be clued into the plan. Not that starship tai-chi was really a plan.

I wasn't sure whether to take it as a vote of confidence or pure foolishness on the part of my crew, but nobody questioned my orders. Instead, they reacted as I reacted, instinctively.

Even trapped within a cone of enemy starships, space is big and three dimensions offer a range of directional choices that old-time fighters could only dream of. Fortunately, I'd learned my kung fu in Mjolnir's miniscule gravity. Fighting in three dimensions was old hat for me.

We veered when Harding's missiles approached—and used the presence of his other ships to trigger the missile's A.I.'s IFF (Identify Friend or Foe) and disarm them.

We retreated from the big but slow forts and poked our missiles at the more mobile but less armored destroyers that constituted the bulk of Harding's force.

After a few moments, first Nara, then Ronin caught the pattern. I noticed them sending missiles not toward the enemy ships, but toward empty places where those ships would go—once I'd completed my next turn.

A groan, maybe from Ronin, followed by an almost physical twist in my gut practically pulled me from the dance. One of our ships, its pilots inexperienced girls, hadn't threaded the gauntlet. Now it vented its atmosphere.

I had to make an extreme effort of will to stay in the moment rather than let myself mourn over the girls I'd sent to their deaths.

"They would have died if you'd done nothing," Shena said. "At least this way ..."

She trailed off, probably because there wasn't a good ending to that sentence. At least this way they'd cost Security some missiles rather than just composting? Was that good enough? I didn't think so.

"Stay with the dance." I called out the next course change.

When fighting multiple opponents, the kung fu master learns to string them out in a line, making them interfere with one another, allowing only one to get a shot at a time. In the old days on Earth, navies had adopted the same tactic, trying to cross the T where the broadsides of all their ships can bear on the enemy while the enemy can fire only one or two bow chasers. It doesn't work as well in three dimensions because the enemy can line up vertically as well as horizontally. Still, I found I'd done exactly that, each zig and zag forcing Harding's forces to respond to my initiative.

Nara and Ronin were doing good work, taking out several attackers and making the others hold back and pop missiles at us rather than close the distance and eliminate us with their heavier energy weapons. The countless hours Shena had spent on the simulators paid off as she deflected more missiles than I'd imagined existed in the galaxy.

Ultimately, though, we couldn't win—especially as the remaining Security ships orbiting Njold lit up and joined the pursuit.

I tweaked my phone to signal the whole ship's company. "All hands," I said, "First, it's been an honor serving with you. You've done your duty and have set an example that will live long after us. Second, I want everyone to double-check your rebreathers now. If you're alive, you can continue the battle against slavery even if you're captured. That is all."

I looked at Ronin. Tears had escaped each of his eyes but his gaze was far away as he plotted trajectories for the last of our missiles.

I reached out and squeezed his biceps. He'd added a few kilos in the weeks we'd spent together—in all the right places. "Thanks," I said.

"We aren't done yet."

"Nope. Not yet."

We were, though, in the final act of the dance, the crescendo.

The *Star* shook like a Hasro user with bad implants as Shena gave everything she had to the rail guns and I shifted ship energy from the engines to the defenses—it wasn't as if we had any place to go.

Still, the incoming missiles were getting closer. Someone, possibly Harding himself, had figured out the dance and was mimicking Ronin, firing not at us but at where we had to go.

I wanted to tell my friends how much I appreciated all they'd done but was out of words.

I wanted to kiss Ronin again, but that was silly.

Instead, I called out the last course correction. A zag back toward the heavy forts when Harding would probably expect me to continue toward the destroyers … because only an idiot would put herself within range of the big forts' energy weapons.

"What the heck?" Nara's always-calm voice was a squeal.

From all over the battlefield, new energy sources registered.

"Why would Harding hide all those ships until now?" Ronin demanded.

Except Harding's ships were taking hits, venting air, and then running.

"It's Earth-Fleet." Shena's voice was filled with wonder. "They one-upped Harding's trap."

"About time they got here." Nara sounded anything but grateful.

"Yeah to both," I said. "What do you say we try to stay alive for the next ten minutes, then talk about whether Noomis was brilliant or a jerk?"

****

Admiral Noomis didn't look especially proud of herself considering she'd achieved a historic victory at very little cost to Earth-Fleet.

She'd asked me, along with my senior officers, to join her and Fleet's Captains, in the fort-like ship she'd captured from Security.

From the second she'd asked us to be seated at a huge round table, it was obvious this meeting was about us.

After all, Earth-Fleet was in good shape considering they'd just won a battle. Their losses had been minimal because Security had basically flown into their target areas. With the defeat of Security's armada, drawn out of position and exposed by their attempts to hunt down the *Blood Star*, Fleet had taken over Security's remaining orbital forts and then sold them to Njold—making it a much harder nut to crack should Security attempt to take up the siege in the future. In return for the array of orbital forts, Njold deeded Bergthora, the second water-bearing planet in the system, as well as dozens of gallons of human blood per week for Fleet's sick sailors.

So, it was a victory.

"Your observations," Noomis said, "made it clear that Harding was hiding something. Security was sending too many supply ships for the number of destroyers and forts in system. Obviously they were laying a trap for Fleet—a trap I couldn't afford to trip."

"So, you left it to us to trip it."

She nodded. "You have an uncanny ability to frustrate ex-Admiral Harding. I hoped that, as well as your incredible luck, would serve ... as it did.

"That doesn't help the crew of *Broken Chain*." We'd picked up the survivors of our lost ship, but more than half had perished.

She shook her head. "You think I sent you ahead because I wanted you to take the losses and to save Fleet. But suppose I had sent a

Fleet squadron. Harding never would have sprung his trap on a handful of Fleet ships. He'd have waited for us to fully commit and those fortresses would have shredded us even if we'd won. For him, though, you're an itch he couldn't scratch. You've got his ships, his first command, and you keep turning up just when he thinks he has everything under control. He doesn't react logically to you. I confess I used that."

"And you couldn't tell me what you were doing?"

She shrugged. "You had to act naturally."

I shrugged, too. Under Noomis's orders, Earth-Fleet had flown countless sorties looking for survivors, and ultimately victims, from *Broken Chain*. And I had been the one who'd insisted we relieve the siege on Njold which Noomis had done. I couldn't fault Noomis for developing a plan that minimized losses and maximized impact. That didn't mean I liked it.

"So," I said, "you have what you want. Your own planet, a source of food, a source of blood, trading routes to pay for what Fleet needs to keep running."

"And two systems where slavery has been banned," she added.

I hadn't forgotten that.

"So," I pretended to ignore her interruption. "This is where we go our separate ways."

"Not … necessarily."

Her tone warned me she was about to spring another surprise. Well, obviously she was better at traps than Harding.

"You want to join the crusade to end slavery?"

She shook her head. "Before, your ex-slaves had no place to go and you were stuck with piracy as your only option. With us, and our new bases, that's changed. We need more workers to complete the renovation of Mjolnir. We need trading ships, and while your pirate ships aren't optimized for trade, they're better than Fleet. We need new sailors and officers to replace those who want to feel dirt beneath their feet now that it's a possibility."

I realized my mouth had dropped open and slammed it shut. It was a good offer. We could live normal lives, work responsible jobs. Piracy, despite the romance, wasn't a long-term career.

Sitting on either side of me, Ronin and Shena both stiffened. Clearly they hadn't expected this offer.

"You're saying I can go home?" Cassie was first to break the silence.

Noomis shook her head. "Although our interference was intended to benefit Plautus as well as Fleet, that planet's leadership feels a certain resentment. They've made it clear that they will not accept the return of any pirates."

"But I never wanted to be a pirate!"

"We need medical technicians in Fleet. The work you've done with your infirmary leads me to believe you would fit."

I was impressed that Noomis knew who Cassie was—or that her implant was good enough to bring up that information.

"We'll purchase any of your ships at full market value," Noomis continued. "Which is about four times more than you were getting before."

"That's a very fair offer," I said.

"But you're not taking it?"

"I didn't say that." I hadn't said it, but it was true. Maybe I was just full of my importance, but I wasn't ready to give up my war on slavery.

"I'll let each of my sailors make their own decision. As for me, there are still millions of girls, across hundreds of worlds, who are being treated like toys by rich perverts too jaded to find real relationships with other humans and too perverse to simply buy a sex-bots. Frankly, there's no way I'll live long enough to end that slavery but until Security or someone else manages to kill me, I'm going to keep trying."

"And I am too." Shena slammed a small fist down on the table. Then again, she knew me. She'd have guessed that I'd do my best to find someplace safe for her.

"Count me in," Nara said.

"Me too," Ronin growled. I wondered if his voice had gotten lower lately.

I'd halfway expected Ronin to jump ship—ever since we'd shared that kiss, the two of us had avoided spending time together unless we were sure someone else would be there. Instead, he was signing up.

I looked at Cassie. "Fleet sounds like a perfect—"

"Oh, bull. I'm already damned. I might as well do some good." If I'd been unsure about Ronin, I thought I'd known exactly what Cassie would do. And staying with me hadn't even been on the possibilities list.

I stood. "Unless there's something else, I'll get back to my squadron and discuss it with my crews."

Noomis also stood. "There is one other thing."

She grabbed me tight before I could react, her Earth-grav acclimated muscles squeezing me so hard I felt my bones bend beneath her strength.

It took me a second to realize this was a hug rather than an attack.

"Although Fleet does not intend to interfere with systems beyond Asgard and Njold," she said, "we share your disgust and horror with the institution of slavery imposed by the corporations who dominate the outer systems. You will always be welcome at any system controlled by us, and Earth's anti-slavery league has asked me to present you this award."

The award was a diamond-incrusted medal to be worn around the neck. Considering that I could have programmed a maintenance bot to churn out a hundred kilo diamond, I wasn't too impressed by the rocks. I also wasn't impressed that all they'd managed to do was send me a medal instead of more pirate ships. Which I told Noomis.

"Earth's anti-slavery league is big on talking and awards," the admiral admitted. "They—"

"Hey," Nara interrupted. "I'm—"

"I haven't forgotten you, Lieutenant Foss," Noomis said. "E.A.L. asked me to apologize for their decision to throw you out for disobeying orders."

"Oh?"

"Well, thank the Anti-Slavery League for this," I tossed the medal to Ronin. "And let them know that we intend to earn a lot more."

Noomis laughed. "I'll do that."

****

Half the girls decided to take Noomis's offer, leaving me enough sailors to crew the *Blood Star* and a corvette I got from Noomis in exchange for our freighters.

I expected Ronin to jump at the chance to be her captain, but he refused. Ultimately, I persuaded Nara to take it.

Noomis insisted on replacing all of the missiles we'd expended in our doomed fight against Security, and we spent a month in orbit around Njold while our repair-bots pulled the *Star* back together.

Then I gathered what was left of my crew.

"First," I said, "I want to thank you for choosing to stay and fight. Because I'm a vampire, I never could fit with station-side society, but none of you are in that situation. You could have been, if not rich, at least comfortable with your share of our prizes. Second, you need to know that we can't win. Even if we escape Security, there are a million slaves in the outer systems, with more being sold every day—we could free a hundred slaves a day for the rest of our lives and we'd still be behind. And Security won't be easy to escape. Rumor is that Harding lost his job, but that just means Security will appoint smarter people to hunt us down.

"Although we can't win, we haven't been caught yet. We have freed over five hundred girls and some boys, too. I think we can free more, maybe lots more, before we get caught. That's all I have to say."

Ronin broke the silence. "That isn't all *I* have to say. I say that you're not sticking with the pirates because you're a vampire, you're sticking with us because it's the right thing to do. And it doesn't bother me that you think about sucking my blood when I kiss you."

I met his eyes. "It doesn't?"

"Okay, maybe it's a little weird. But hey, it's not like I'm not sort of weird, too."

"Eeew," Shena said. "Shouldn't we be planning our next raid? I mean, you can do that kissy stuff on your own time, when the rest of us don't have to watch."

"There isn't going to be any kissy stuff," I said.

"Are you sure?"

"Uh …" I glanced around and saw that my friends were mostly snickering. "Ares sector is a huge market for pre-teen girls, and since it doesn't hire Security Corporation, they might not be ready for us. I thought we'd see if we could raise the price of doing business for them."

"Okay." Shena giggled. "Now that that's decided, why don't you go and kiss?"

"Because…"

"Sounds like a good idea to me." Ronin grinned at me.

"That's because you're a boy."

"Yep."

I wasn't going to kiss him again … not right away, anyway. But the thought had a definite appeal.

Books by Rob Preece

Hot in the Saddle
Hunger
In the Werewolf's Den
Kingmaker
Medium in the Middle
Merchant Prince of Arcadia
Nano-Corporate
One Handsome Devil
A Really Bad Hair Day
The School for Monsters and Misfits
Veil of the Goddess